Verge 2020

Verge 2020

Ritual

Edited by Rebecca Bryson, Benjamin Jay
and Giulia Mastrantoni

MONASH
UNIVERSITY
PUBLISHING

Verge 2020: Ritual

Monash University Publishing
Matheson Library Annexe
40 Exhibition Walk
Monash University
Clayton, Victoria 3800, Australia
www.publishing.monash.edu

Monash University Publishing brings to the world publications which advance the
best traditions of humane and enlightened thought.

Monash University Publishing titles pass through a rigorous process of independent
peer review.

ISSN: 2208-5637

ISBN: 9781925835847 (paperback)
ISBN: 9781925835861 (pdf)
ISBN: 9781925835854 (epub)

www.publishing.monash.edu/books/verge2020-9781925835847.html

Series: Verge: Creative Writing

Design: Les Thomas

Cover image: Photo by Curology on Unsplash

A catalogue record for this book is available from the National Library of Australia.

Contents

HIGHEST-PLACING
MONASH UNIVERSITY STUDENT
IN THE MONASH PRIZE

Victor Chrisnaa Senthinathan

Acknowledgements

First and foremost, the editors of *Verge* would like to acknowledge the people of the Kulin Nations as the Traditional owners of the land on which this publication was created. We pay our respects to Elders past, present and emerging, and acknowledge Aboriginal and Torres Strait Islanders as the first people of Australia. They have never ceded sovereignty, and remain strong in their enduring connection to land and culture. We have immense gratitude that we were able to curate the *Verge* stories on this stolen land, and are forever indebted.

We thank the following people for extending their time, efforts and assistance in making this publication a possibility:

Dr Ali Alizadeh, *Verge* Coordinator
Assoc Prof Kevin Foster, Head of School of Languages, Literatures, Cultures & Linguistics
Joanne Mullins & Les Thomas, Monash University Publishing
Izzy Roberts-Orr, Artistic Director & Co-CEO of Emerging Writers' Festival
Alice Muhling, Executive Director of Emerging Writers' Festival
Calvin Fung, Former Editor of *Verge* and *Colloquy*
Gavin Yates, Former Editor of *Verge*
Alice Davies & Sally Riley, Monash University
Staff at the Faculty of Arts, Monash University
Staff at the School of Languages, Literatures, Cultures & Linguistics, Monash University

Our complete and utter gratitude goes to the following peer reviewers, whose expertise and critical eyes were very appreciated by the editors and contributors alike:

Dr Sergio Alcides
Dr Benjamin Andreo
Dr Gero Bauer
Dr Brooke Collins-Gearing
Dr Joanne Elliott

Dr Ali Alizadeh
Dr Daniel Baker
Dr Bonny Cassidy
Dr Linda Daley
Associate Professor Enza Gandolfo

Associate Professor Jespel Gulddal   Dr Luigi Gussago
Dr John Hawke   Dr Laura Lori
Dr Rebecca Jones   Dr Brigid Magner
Dr Helen Marshall   Dr Sascha Morrell
Dr Chris Murray   Dr David Musgrave
Dr Richard Newsome   Dr Catherine Padmore
Dr Sana Peden   Dr Juliane Roemhild
Dr Aisling Smith   Dr Michelle J. Smith
Associate Professor Rebecca Suter   Dr Chris Watkin
Associate Professor Jessica Wilkinson   Dr Chris Worth

Special thanks to those who offered all kinds of support, including moral and emotional:

Daniel Steen
Joshua Morris
Alessandra Turriziani & Egidio Mastrantoni

And last, but most certainly not least, a huge thanks to all the contributors. Without you, this book would not exist and would certainly not contain all of the brilliant and imaginative pieces that lie within its covers. We wish you the absolute best for your future creative endeavours and hope that you will always be able to carve out a space in the world for your wonderful, weird and wild writing.

Rebecca Bryson
Benjamin Jay
Giulia Mastrantoni

Foreword

Birthdays, weddings, funerals, cooking a first meal for someone we love, cracking the champagne to celebrate an achievement. Then, there are the small rituals. We begin each of our days with a ritual. Whether it's rolling over to turn off an alarm, scrolling through Instagram, taking a few moments of silence before the day roars to life, reading the news; or, something that is so completely automatic that we don't even give it any thought, like going through the motions of washing our faces, drying our bodies or brushing our teeth. It's the culmination of these small rituals that get us through the day before we return to our homes and ourselves and complete the small rituals that bring us to sleep, only to wake up and do it all over again. There are rituals that mark the beginning – the start of a new year or a marriage. There are rituals that mark an ending, like lowering a body into the ground, but ultimately will enable us to complete that part of our life and leave room to tend to another small bud. Through ritual comes growth.

When we stumbled upon this year's theme for *Verge* during a brainstorming session, we knew we had hit upon something rich with possibility; the issue would surely grow into something really special. We were astounded by the high quality of submissions for this issue, and the wide interpretation of the theme. We were hoping that the theme would inspire all different sorts of creative outputs – speculative, fantasy, realist, absurd, heartbreaking, joyful, hilarious, baffling – and we were right to think it would hit a chord with writers. This issue is the culmination of thirty-four brilliant authors' experiences with rituals, through poetry, creative non-fiction and short fiction. We, as editors, created our own rituals through curating this collection. Reading each submission, working with the authors to lightly shape each piece, ensuring consistency and flow. And we know that you, the reader, will be enjoying this issue as part of *your* ritual – taking time from your day to indulge in wonderful creative writing.

The Editors

1

Old Mate

Richie Black

As soon as I heard the news, I knew I had to be there for Dave. It's what mates do. Those bonds are ya know, *sacred*, I 'spose – or something. Of course, Raelene says it's just an excuse to get on the piss – merely demonstrating her ignorance, again.

Gotta plane to Sydney and when I get to his place, Dave staggers out of the garage toward me. Says Chicko thanks for coming down etcetera. Hugs me tight. This big fucking ex-tradie (he's in real estate now) welling up.

Bit overwhelming – so I go, you alright matey – and then he's croaking about how the prognosis ain't good. *No good*, we're *fucked*.

We go in and, en route, Dave grabs a can from the fridge in the garage for us both (good ol' Dave).

The house turns out to be heaving with women (thank god I'm here for Dave!) – Clem's sisters and her daughters. She's been brought home, from the hospital to, well, ya know.

I recognise Steph, Clem and Dave's youngest, from when she was a sprog – she gives me the evils when I step inside. Can't take it personally, she's obviously got a lot on her plate – so I give her a hug and tell her that everything's going to be okay. She kind of pushes me away, and says, no it won't.

Asks me what I'm doing here and I say, just supporting a mate in his time of grief – and she says something like, she's not dead yet – and walks away.

Que sera, I think.

I also recognise Clem's sister Anne – we went around together for a bit when we were younger. She's a bit worn around the edges these days but aren't we all.

Then Dave says you should say hello to Clem, so we go into the bedroom. She looks like hell. All shrivelled up and bald as a coot from the chemo, just wisps of hair left. Rasping away through a puckered-up mouth.

I dunno if she's awake, but big Dave's got on his knees next to the bed and whispers at her that Chicko is here. Funny thing is, Clem and I never really got on – but I go over, and say hi Clem, how ya doin', which is a pretty stupid thing to say come to think of it but whaddya do.

She doesn't register anyway.

I reckon she should be in hospital but of course I stay shtum.

So we're standing around the bed not saying anything suddenly. Pretty grim. So I says to Dave, why don't we go to the pub, mate. Get away for a bit.

Dunno if he heard me initially, he's just staring at Clem – but then he mumbles, yeah righto, without taking his eyes off her.

So we're heading out of the door and we pass the kitchen where Steph is mashing up some fruit for her mum – and she goes where you two off to? And Dave says, just to the pub for a couple.

Nada in reply, of course.

We're driving in his truck and he says, Chicko – you got a place to stay? I make a half-arsed suggestion that I'll get a room at the Gladstone – but I know Dave. True to form, he says you can stay on me couch.

We get into the Glad and it's basically the same – despite a few bodge attempts at a renovation – still has all the atmos' of a casino at about three am in the morning, bless.

A couple of the familiar reprobates drift into our orbit – Muzz, Alby and Brett.

Hello Chicko – how are ya?

Not bad.

Dave, how's Clem?

Not good.

After a few commiserating bevs, Dave says, you boys wanna come back to mine? Gotta fridge full of piss.

Rightio – we all get into his truck.

So we're soon rolling back into the driveway at Casa Dave. I'm a little leery of the reception committee but Dave says we'll keep the noise down. Nevertheless, a few cans later, it gets a bit jolly on the patio – Dave's so pissed he's laughing at *everything*. I'm maggot too, so I totally forget there's poor Clem dying of cancer only a few feet away in her bedroom.

That's until Steph comes out and tells us to shut-up – have some respect!

Fuck me, Dave looks like a scolded kid.

She's a piece of work. Case in point, I'm in the kitchen one day helping myself to a bit of the lunch spread the ladies have prepared – and I'm saying Dave seems to be struggling and Steph just goes how long are you here for? I say, I'm here as long as Dave needs me, and the response is: *you're just enabling his drinking problem*.

Charming.

Anyway, at least I've got Anne on side, I think – turns out she's newly single. She'll come out and have a dart on the patio and we'll have a bit of a chinwag.

She talks a bit about the old days running about with Clem and how she already misses her. She says she's happy in a funny way – that they've brought her sister home. Clem's amongst her people, in the house she bought with Dave, the home she loved, the kinda place she'd dreamt of all her life.

It's like a vigil, Anne says, the family – the sisters and their kids – are coming together in a way they've not done in literally years.

Funny how good things happen in the worst of times.

And I say I feel like part of the family, gathering around Dave. Anne gives me a bit of a smile but it's gone quick. She's doing it tough, poor thing. I'm thinking she might be looking for comfort (don't tell Raelene).

Clem's literally got days, according to the nurse that comes and goes.

The tension's obviously getting to Dave. I think a bit about what Steph said – but, you gotta remember, we each deal with grief in our own way.

The women have their fussy little lunch rituals and stuff – and we have our own thing.

Still, he does look a bit unwell. Sorta red and bloated. I notice he doesn't wear shoes anymore, just thongs, cos his feet have swollen up so big.

There's plans for the extended family to swing around for lunch on Sunday. Anne reckons the end is nigh. They can sense it.

Part of me thinks I should piss off – but I didn't want to leave Dave alone with the in-laws. Besides which, Anne is making her famous fish pie.

As it turns out, it's all a non-issue, cos while I'm taking it easy on the patio, Dave comes steaming out of the house.

Come on mate, let's go to the pub, he says.

On the drive, I ask what's up and he says his daughter called him a drunk. Then Dave says, and they think you're just hanging around for free piss and food. Called you – *me* – a scab.

Bloody hell. Bit of a slur on the ol' honour.

By ten pm he's pretty loose – and the Glad staff tell him no more. Nevertheless, he insists on driving. Straight to da bottle-o.

Hands me his wallet – says grab another case.

I think it's probably my shout but then I did fork out a bit for the plane ticket.

The house is dark inside, the sisters have gone to bed in spare rooms out back. Steph's keeping watch on Clem.

She means well, says Dave. But it's hopeless.

Hopeless.

He keeps repeating it.

You need a can, I say.

We get through a few and then – … well, to be honest, it all gets hazy. Dave's in a state – taking his clothes off in the lounge cos he thinks he's in his bedroom.

Eventually he passes out in his undies on the lounge. I go to sleep on the other sofa. Nighty-night.

Suddenly there's light and being shaken awake –

I go, piss off, I'm sleeping –

But I realise it's Anne who's grabbing me arm – and for a moment, I'm thinking, *hello darlin'*, but then she says, Clem has just passed.

Farrrrk.

She says, you've got to wake him up and tell him.

And there's Dave in his undies snoring like a jack-hammer on the sofa. I go, I can't tell him that – it'll kill him. She says, he needs to know.

Then she says, how did you let him get into this state?

Me? He's grieving and I was there for him!

She mutters something about letting him drink himself to death.

What the f—

But she just leaves.

Sod ya then.

I go over to the big man and he's a mess – he's... well, he's pissed himself. I try to wake him. Finally I see these two bloodshot eyes open up.

Chicko, what up?

And I go to him as gently as I can, mate, it's Clem – she's passed away.

And I think, that should rouse him but he's still too pissed. It doesn't register. I say it again, and there's a flicker of acknowledgement – then his eyes just roll back.

So, whaddyado? I make a coffee. Real black.

Eventually the nurse arrives and one of Dave's grandkids – must've been asleep out back – wanders into the lounge and, of course, clocks the whole bloody scene.

What's wrong with Grandad?

I dunno mate, I say (and piss off will ya, I think).

Meantime, muggins is trying to get Dave to drink the coffee who's complaining there's no sugar in it. I tell him to drink it you idiot, your wife is dead, and he takes a big swig – and, of course, he pukes it up again. For f—k's sake Dave you idiot! – and that little sprog is still standing right behind me gawping away.

Suddenly the big man's lurching upwards, so I go steady on mate, put some pants on and he's just slurring, I've got to see her, got to make sure she's alright blah blah.

And he staggers towards the bedroom – I follow him in and, gawd, there's a lot of family around the bed where Clem is.

So there's Dave standing in the doorway, looking down at her, in his y-fronts, Steph staring at him – and just says all quiet to me *make yourself useful for once and get that fuckwit out of her*e.

I look at her and I'm about to arc right up at the little… but Dave's *gone* anyway, back to the lounge room and I find him flopped back in the vom and piss on the sofa, snoring his head off, his wife dead in the other room, and it's about now I'm thinking Steph's right, the silly old bastard probably does have an issue with the booze.

Christ knows, I'll be there for him. Well, as long as I can. At least for the funeral. Won't be able to hang around too long after. Gotta get back to work, 'course, plus I've got a mate – Trev – having his buck's weekend in a fort-night. Third bloody marriage, can you believe it? Glutton for punishment, that one! It'll be back in Bris-vegas, so yeah, I'll go home for that.

Should be a good time – and, besides, he's a mate.

2

Are You Troubled by the Following?

Derek Chan

Do you worry excessively about dirt, germs, or chemicals?

I believe I am beautiful   only because they said so
in the hospital   while I was being scrubbed clean
of my mother   I still believe I am beautiful when I chip
away my skin with a pine-cone   lemon peel bursting
in brain stem   until I finally find the crystal shards
laced delicately around my bone   glimmering
like rainbow trout skin   and I know I am

Do you have unwanted ideas, images, or impulses that seem silly, nasty, or horrible?

Even a dog digs up its owner on the sixth day
of mourning   to feed on the hand it once fed off
        it's impossible to tell hunger from love
so of course I will never kill someone in my sleep
  even though I have heard it is possible
        please wake me up
the dogs are eating your sister

Are there thoughts you must think repeatedly to feel comfortable or ease anxiety?

With butterflies for hands   everything I touch ripples like a shredded flag
today you drop a watercolour onto concrete   tomorrow a beautiful monarch
butterfly drops dead   like two bright blue hands tossed onto quicksand
I suppose only God understands the significance of the 6th cereal box starting
from the back of the shelf the old men can say what they want to say about me
I think what I want   I think what I want to think what I want I think I want
to think what I want to think I think I want to think what   I want to think

Do you wash yourself or things around you excessively?

If cleanliness is next to godliness then I would like to be packed
into a washing machine and sent spinning through space
and when I land on Pluto   I will emerge with a halo
of underwear   hailed as an angel
        a lighthouse brighter than its light

Are you always afraid you will lose something of importance?

As a young boy
      my appetite for beauty
was infamous. My tonsils a colony
of diamonds,
      arteries pulsing
with rubies, rainbows
      spilling from
fingernails
As a child I swallowed a quail egg
      whole and warm.
Even now I desperately
      gulp nests of warm duck down
for a sign of life.
      I can bear to lose
almost anything. Just please
not this.
      The moon
inside my belly.

3

Blaze

Anna McShane-Potts

Rather than the baby crying, as she often does, it's the smell of smoke that wakes me in the middle of the night. We had opened the window behind our bed a little, to allow an airflow through the bedroom, and a thin stream of smoke finds its way in through the crack. I can see it clearly, it's illuminated by a red glow that is coming in from outside.

I wake Marcus when I slam the window shut, trying to keep the smoke out. Together we go outside to the front of the house to see what's happening. On opening the door we are greeted by a wall of heat. The street is full of smoke and flashing lights, people yelling, neighbours craning over their picket fences. (They're careful not to step beyond their gates because in doing so they'd have to help.)

The people from the house across the street are huddling together on the footpath, clutching each other as they watch firefighters hose down their home. Marcus runs inside to get a blanket and takes it out to the family, staying with them to make sure they're okay. Me, I go back inside and close the front door to stop the smoke from filling our house (I know it can't be healthy for the baby), and I stand in the front room, watching through the window.

* * *

When Marcus finally comes back in (it is not long before he will have to start getting ready for work) I force him into the shower, demanding that he wash the smoke from his hair and skin. I throw his clothes into the washing machine and pour the liquid soap over them, in the hope of getting rid of the smell. When he gets out of the shower I sniff his hair for smoke and send him back in.

* * *

I have to take our quilt to the dry cleaners. The smoke that came in through our window got into the down. When I step outside in the morning to get into the car the street still reeks of smoke; it clings to my clothing and hair, the baby's too. I decide to park in the garage (which we very rarely do) from now on, to avoid having to step outside again. Unfortunately, when I get the quilt back that afternoon I can still smell the lingering scent of ash – so I have to throw it away after all.

Marcus comes home from work early that evening. I can tell he's home not because I hear him arrive, but because of the smell of smoke that has followed him inside. I think he can tell by the look on my face when he walks into the kitchen, because he turns straight around to go to the shower.

* * *

Marcus has started to get angry with me. It's been three weeks since the fire and I still won't let him open any windows. He is complaining that we're spending too much on air-conditioning. I can tell he's also getting sick of having to shower the minute he gets home and having to wear slightly damp shirts to work because I'm washing them so often. But what choice do we have? The street still smells too bad to allow the air to get into the house.

* * *

I wake late one Saturday morning to find Marcus standing with a cup of coffee in the open French doors. I scream at him, flying across the room. I drag him inside before slamming them closed. I am so furious I start crying, but when he moves to embrace me I have to push him away, he smells too smoky. He gets mad at me again and goes into another room.

* * *

Marcus thinks it might be a good idea if the baby and I spend a bit of time at his parents' holiday shack in the country. It's a one-bedroom wooden cabin, set among tall eucalypts and tufts of dry grass. I am sure we are surrounded by snakes and spiders, and getting from the car to the shack I keep a careful distance from any possible hiding place. There is a nest of bull ants by the steps to the front door and, babe in arms, I have to leap over them in my heeled boots.

Inside, the shack is dark, its walls lined with rough sawn wooden slats. There is a fireplace in the corner that I eye warily, before throwing a thick rug over the metal fire guard to obscure it from view.

* * *

I think the baby likes going on walks. Maybe she likes the smell of the eucalypts. Sometimes, because it's so dry and hot here, I think I can smell their leaves burning and I look up into the canopy to check, but they never are.

I spend the evenings cooking and reading to the baby. I ask Marcus to bring more books when he visits on the weekend – we have gone through each one six or seven times already, not that the baby seems to mind.

When Marcus arrives, he brings the smell of the smoke with him. It cascades out of the car and lingers around the driveway. I try not to say anything, knowing how angry he will be, and I've had such a pleasant time at the shack that I don't want us to argue. But soon I can't stand it anymore and I ask him to put on some old clothes from the cupboard so I can wash the ones he has brought. He isn't happy, but I can tell he doesn't want to fight either.

We have a lovely weekend together before Marcus has to go back for work. Several times I think I can smell burning when we go for walks, but I look around and see nothing, so I don't mention it.

* * *

It's just two days later and something is definitely burning. I can sense it the moment I wake. In trepidation I look out the window to the bright morning – but I see nothing. I decide to go outside to look, but when I open the door the smell is so appalling that I slam it shut. It is strange that I can't see the smoke, I have no doubt that it's there.

* * *

The baby won't stop crying. I think the cabin fever is getting to us both; we haven't been outside in four days now. But the good news is that I have discovered where the smoke is coming from.

It's the clouds! They look normal at first, small grey wisps floating above us. But on closer inspection they are actually much lower than normal, and they are more translucent, like smoke. Yes, it is definitely coming from the sky.

I actually think they're getting even lower, moving closer towards us.

I know that the baby isn't happy, but we can't go outside now. It just wouldn't be safe.

* * *

I tell Marcus that we're both sick and he shouldn't come this weekend. 'Don't come,' I say. 'We can't afford you getting sick and missing work.' He seems worried, but I tell him it is just a cold and he listens to me and eventually agrees.

We are not unwell, of course; I just don't want him to come. I know how shocked he would be if he saw what I have done to the shack.

The curtains are all tightly drawn across the windows, and I have used duct tape to attach the edges to the walls so there are no gaps. I leave only one curtain free, so I can check the sky every morning. I have used Blu-Tack to fill the locks to the doors, and stuffed old clothing into the gaps underneath them so that smoke can't get in. It's awfully dark in here when the lights are turned off – even during the day.

* * *

The smoke is even lower now, it is brushing against the tops of the trees.

* * *

I wake to find myself bathed in sweat. My bedroom is boiling – there surely must be fire outside.

I try to check outside but have to back away from the window the glass is so hot. I run to the kitchen where I fill buckets and containers with water, before filling the sink too, just in case there is a fire.

And of course the baby won't stop crying, I am getting very worried about her.

* * *

I think there is smoke in the cabin, I can smell it faintly whenever I move quickly and disturb the air. The poor baby, there isn't much I can do. I try to fashion a face mask for both of us, like the ones they use in hospitals that cover the nose and mouth, to protect us from breathing in anything harmful.

I can tell she doesn't like it much.

* * *

It's getting difficult to see in here, the rooms are so hazy from the smoke.

I finally call Marcus and tell him to come, but I worry that it will be too late by the time he gets here.

* * *

I read to the baby under a small lamp by the couch. I am worried about having anything electrical on, fearing that it might start a fire, but if I don't read the baby drives me crazy with all the crying. So I turn on only the smallest lamp when I have to.

* * *

We have just started a new book when the room suddenly seems much lighter.

The globe beside me is getting brighter, light coming not just from the thin wires inside, but filling the entire bulb. I can suddenly read the words to the story much more clearly. And it's not just the one bulb, it is happening all around the room. They look like tiny little balls of fire that are sure to explode at any moment.

I then look across to the kitchen to see flames pouring out of the taps above the sink. I set the baby down and rush over, quickly turning on the taps so that water comes out of them at full force, smothering the fire. The sink is overflowing, soaking the kitchen floor, but at least the flames have stopped.

I look back into the main room as small red specks start to appear on the curtains, burning patches into the fabric. And then they too are alight.

I pick up the baby and we stand in the corner as the fire breaks out in different places across the room. The door is covered in flames. The table, the chairs, the kitchen bench – all burning bright red.

The baby doesn't seem too worried, which I am thankful for. You would think she would be screaming from the intolerable heat and from fear of the flames, but she doesn't seem to mind at all. In fact, she's gurgling away merrily in my arms.

She smiles up at me, and from the corner of her mouth I think I see a wisp of something grey float out. She laughs, and deep inside her I see a red glow.

She starts to get hot in my hands, as hot as the fire burning around me. She giggles, and flames spurt out from between her lips.

I am panicking, holding my burning baby in my arms.

I run to the kitchen and plunge the baby into the sink. The water sizzles when her body touches it, and I have to keep her completely submerged until she cools enough for the bubbling to stop.

* * *

I can feel the flames receding behind me, the heat at the back of my neck cools, the smoke burning my eyes disappears.

I look down at my baby. From beneath the surface she's watching me peacefully. When Marcus arrives he will be able to pick her up from the water and take her home.

He shouldn't be long now.

4

Christmas in October

Ava Redman

'Are you fucking kidding me?!'

I blinked from one side of the aisle to the other, zig-zagging my gaze like at a tennis match. On one side was the orange and black – pumpkins and skeletons – while the other side was glitzy green glitter trees and all things tinsel. It was only the first week of October and department stores were stocking the garbage like it was Clean the Beach week!

'I'm so over this,' I groaned as I watched curious bystanders become pawns in the great economical debate as they neared the glittery horrors like flies drawn to cow pat.

I exited the Dollar shop trying to rid myself of the plastic snow and cobwebs.

As I entered Kmart, I almost exhaled in relief, until I caught sight of the shitstorm that was Halloween and Christmas vying for my attention and in the eye of the storm was a monument that deserved to be destroyed.

He was two metres tall, holding a digital sign that read *75 days till Christmas*. Fucking giant blow-up Santa.

I flipped him off as I marched past, seeking out the stationary aisle. It was always a feat not to yell at the machines at checkout. *'Please take your items.'*

'Give me a fucking sec?' Forcing my hessian bag to swallow my pens and paper. What were we now but people who only had permission to shop when they brought their own bags and the damn machines wouldn't allow extra time delay before you picked up your items or put away your money? What happened to more hands make light work?

I suppose I'm just trying to explain the lead up to how I assaulted Santa Claus. Not the real one, he only pops up on coke ads now. I mean the giant blow up Santa. It was a crime of passion, as I marched up to him and kicked him like a child kicks an adult in the shins. I was out of the store just as the attendants were milling around the fallen Santa.

'And that's why we will be shopping at Target this year –'

'You mean, you kicked Santa and now we can't shop at Kmart?' Heather said. 'But all you did was knock over a blow-up Santa. You didn't break anything.'

I twisted my hair around my fingers, biting my lip. 'I mean, I didn't. But I kinda got into a shouting match with the store manager and well, it's easier if we just don't shop there this Christmas. Besides, they have a poor selection of toys anyway.'

'What? Why am I being punished for your crimes?' Heather threw up her hands, though no one noticed. We'd squeezed into a Gloria Jeans for the limited-edition seasonal drinks and Christmas hits that looped in the background. It was the only time of the year I could tolerate Mariah Carey. It was thirty-five degrees outside and although my loyalty belonged to independent outdoor cafes in Sydney's trendy Inner West, I could easily be sold out for air-con in a franchise café that overcharged and only catered to Asian tourists.

Heather pressed her palm down on the sticky table, her eyes burning into mine. 'I have exactly fifty dollars to spend on ten people and where else can I do that?'

'The Dollar shop?" I swallowed.

Heather threw up her hands and groaned. 'I hate this time of year. I swear I spend every year getting broke between Halloween and Christmas and spending the rest of the year trying to get back in the green again only to get back in the red at the end.'

I took another sip of my cinnamon pumpkin latte savouring every mouthful since it only existed one month of the year. 'Or we could break up with all our close friends and family and reunite with them just in time for Boxing Day sales and get them all make-up gifts at half price.'

Heather sipped her soy gingerbread latte. 'I could produce some paintings and give everyone something I made from scratch with love. Even the cards will be handmade.'

I grimaced. 'Sounds like something only poor people do.'

Heather blinked. 'We are poor people. We can't keep affording these annual holidays society throws on us.'

'Yup,' I eyed her Michael Kors wallet that she swears she bought in a sale. I caught her glance at my Pandora bracelet that I got last month. I fingered the chain to hide the latest pendant… that I'd bought on an impulse, which didn't count right now since I had been suffering from a tough week and I'd earned it.

'What if we take on a nomadic lifestyle and explain that's why we won't be doing gifts this year?' I raised my arms, feeling the weight of Pandora. If this were poker right now, I'd be even more broke than the broke that had gotten us here.

She squealed 'I'm a material girl in a material world! I'm not giving up my basic rights to have shit and to hoard shit that makes no sense.'

'Ok,' I hissed out a breath, massaging my temples in slow circular motions. 'How about we rent out my room for the holidays and I sleep in yours. We can make good money.' I nodded. 'All the yuppies want to see Sydney at Christmas and New Year's.'

'It's Summer. I can barely sleep in thirty degrees as it is and now you want to sleep beside me like a damn heater?!' I opened my mouth, but she cut me off. 'And you snore.' She folded her arms.

'It's a damp house. I don't snore, I have blocked airways, even when it's hot.' Heather still wouldn't make eye contact with me. 'Secret Santa?'

'That's a work thing. Which reminds me. I have to get the new guy Duncan a gift too! Fuck! Fucking Duncan!'

'Should we be holding a garage sale to sell off stuff we don't need?'

'Ooo,' Heather licked the whipped cream off the end of her straw. 'We could try sell that foot spa Mum gave me for Christmas last year, or that acupuncture mat Casey got me. You also have those bath sets that your family keep getting you in your cupboard and a thousand candles.'

'That's because they don't really know me.'

'It would help if you were more decisive when telling them what to get.' She eyed my bracelet, emphasising her point. I wasn't going to voice that talking to my family around the holidays was a stress in and of itself.

'So, your answer is to sell off last year's gifts to buy this year's gifts,' I said.

'Yep, and we'll likely have to do the same next year,' Heather shrugged.

'Vicious cycle,' I voiced. 'But doable.'

We sealed the deal with a high-five and continued sipping from our limited-edition concoctions that neither of us really liked all that much.

5

Mind the Gap. Repeat. Mind the Gap.

Kerrin O'Sullivan

Penelope passes through Embankment tube station each morning on her way to work.

Week-night evenings, she gets off and waits a while on the platform listening to the announcements, rather than going straight home. There's no hurry. No cat to feed, no one to cook for, no rush to get home.

On Saturdays she cleans the Shoreditch apartment she and Humphrey bought together. On Sundays, she buys a bunch of blooms at the flower market to take to Highgate Cemetery. Peonies usually, Humphrey's favourite. Sometimes, instead of making the trip to the cemetery, she puts the flowers in a vase by her bed and detours via Brick Lane to wander amongst the tourists. Those are the days she longs for company, to be swept along, somehow belonging.

No one speaks to her as she sits on the metal bench on the Embankment platform, week-night evenings, her overcoat buttoned ankle to neck, a tartan scarf around her throat – the one Humphrey gave her one Christmas. No one notices her, she could be invisible. It frees her up to do what she comes for, without distraction.

She doesn't court attention. Why would she? What she needs, it's all here.

'*Mind the Gap*,' sounds the clear, authoritative voice on the Underground's Public Address recording. The automatic doors close and another train pulls away. '*Mind the gap*,' Penelope ponders, is it an order? Or simply a suggestion?

Some nights, she's held up at the hospital in Southwark, a full waiting room of patients. An x-ray technician has rung in ill, the MRI machine breaks down, there's an urgent request to see someone not on the list – Penelope will squeeze them in.

'So 'old school',' Humphrey used to tease. 'You actually care!'

She's been a doctor a long time now, knows all too well the anxiety of illness evoked by a lump where it shouldn't be, a shadow on a film, an unexpected pattern on a screen. Even before Humphrey became ill, even before the tumour was diagnosed.

And what's the rush really to get to Embankment, it doesn't matter what time she arrives. Or what time she leaves. She could sit there all night if she wanted.

Penelope chooses the same greenish-grey metal bench. Watches the crowd bunch behind the painted safety line. Feels the blast of air, a sudden sonic boom as the train whooshes into view. Hears the warning, *'Mind the Gap,'* before the doors close and the train accelerates away.

A fluid stream of bodies push towards the exits and escalators. Only Penelope is stationary, listening, remembering. The London Underground's recording – it's a gift to her from the grave, she thinks. Humphrey's deep actor's voice, the words perfectly weighted and paced, *'Mind the Gap'*. His command echoes through the tube station's spaces. Humphrey is speaking to her. She picks her bag up to leave, and sits back down.

One more train, one more announcement, then home. One last chat. A few words from Humphrey.

Just three.

Then home.

6

Cornered

Fiona Murphy

WINNER OF THE MONASH PRIZE

When I started studying anatomy I was daunted by the new vocabulary. The body had become a collection of many small things, each with a specific name. The corners and bumps of bigger more shapely bones, seemingly insignificant and almost accidental looking blimps, were all named. With time, these landmarks would become more obvious when I understood their purpose; I slowly began to learn how to read the geography of bones: the rough patches are where muscles latch on and the shallow indents are passageways allowing blood vessels and nerves to safely transverse the body. Until that knowledge cohered in my own body, I waded through lists of names for the minute and mundane.

A university tutor mentioned that most anatomical terms come from Ancient Latin and Greek. It was comforting to think about the course syllabus as a language: the language of the body. Using exhausting repetition, I slowly learned the new combinations of letters and sounds by rote, until, eventually, they folded into my memory and replaced the words that I used to know for the body – collarbone to clavicle, shoulder blade to scapula, shinbone to tibia, and so on. It took me longer still, years in fact, to realise that these words in their original form were names for simple, everyday objects. For instance, clavicle comes from the classical Latin word *clavicula*, which means 'small key, bolt'. This long thin bone performs an elegant twist whenever the arm lifts, like a key turning in a lock. The scapula is a flattish bone with sharp edges and a pointed tip. Its name is derived from *skap* 'to cut, scrape'. Not only does the shoulder blade resemble a shovel, but it's thought that the scapulas of animals were once used as such, blades for cutting and scraping the earth. Then there's the shinbone. A long and exceedingly straight bone, *tibia* means a pipe or flute. And, for a time, these kinds of wind instruments were also made from bone.

Early anatomists were so keen about naming our bodies after commonplace objects that it was only when they got to a portion of the hip bone that their system came undone. Since the curved and somewhat knobbly bone does not resemble any known object, it was named the *innominate*, which is Latin for 'not named'.

Knowing the origins of these words feels as if the boundaries between our bodies and the world is blurred. The method of naming things is not directed in only one way: as while our bodies are named after commonplace items, our built world has also taken on anatomical terms. A building can have good bones, there can be the heart of a house and roads are the arteries of a city. In considering the poetics of space, or more specifically the form and function of buildings, Gaston Bachelard uses a touchstone phrase – I am the space where I am. So perhaps there aren't even blurred boundaries, but no real division at all.

The languages of buildings and bodies are so overlaid that they are almost circular. How we understand the world is through our bodies and how we understand our bodies is by comparing them to the world. For instance: when the bones of the body meet one another, side by side or end to end, they 'articulate'. This comes from the Latin word *articulatus* ('separated into joints'). The commonplace meaning of articulate, beyond the body, is clear, distinct speech. As if each word in a sentence has been separated into joints. When the bones of a building meet one another, sturdy and upright and angled for loadbearing, they are called joints. And it is in these narrow spaces where walls meet, say in the corner booth of a café or backed up against the wall of a bar, that sound, at least for me, becomes articulate. It is here, the walls do the work of funnelling voices towards me, allowing speech to become distinct and clear. I am the space where I am: on the edges, cornered.

* * *

This relationship between ourselves and the world that we create has become, in modern times, less circular and more consequential – 'First we shape our buildings and afterwards our buildings shape us.' When Winston Churchill said this in 1944, he was being more literal than poetic. He was arguing that the British parliamentary Commons Chamber be restored to an 'adversarial rectangular pattern' after it had been destroyed during the Blitz. At the time, Churchill was eschewing calls for a sweeping circular or horseshoe arrangement favoured by other legislative assemblies. During the debate, Churchill went so far as to suggest that the original shape of the Chamber was 'responsible' for the British two-party system, and so maintaining the narrow, tightly cornered space would be essential for retaining parliamentary democracy. His argument was met with overwhelming support in a free vote. Giles Gilbert Scott, who amongst things designed the red telephone box, was the architect tasked with the job. Now, some seventy years after the Commons Chamber has been reopened, the decision to maintain the historical architecture is still considered to have been the right one, with the parliamentary website stating that 'the confrontational design helps to keep debates lively and robust but also intimate'.

I think about how buildings shape me, the places that cause my body to bend and shrink. To surreptitiously separate from crowds and head for the margins of a room. Seeking corners to tuck myself into. Even when I try to resist tucking myself into a corner, my body still buckles as if being folded into one. Candid photographs, after parties or events, reveal my body contorted in angles of effort, lips folded into a grim line, arms nested in one another as if holding myself firm. In these photographs I see a shell of a thing; alert and watching the external.

I try to imagine what it would be like if all buildings were designed to keep conversations lively and robust. Buildings where I wouldn't need to press myself into walls to avoid sinking in the swell of sound. Large public spaces that would feel intimate by design. Imagine the ease and democracy of it all.

* * *

For as long as I can remember I've woken up early. I suspect that this habit developed as a result of growing up in a large family and a small home. There were six of us and three bedrooms, and so sharing space was a given. I hadn't realised how much of a consideration it was until I moved out of home and into a share house in my early twenties. The room I rented was classified as a study by the real estate agent, and so I moved in without placing my name on the lease. Despite being able to touch either wall with arms outstretched and having to shuffle sideways as my single bed dominated the floor space, the room felt immense and entirely mine. It was then, finally able to lay claim over a space all my own, that I realised that my morning routine had been one of retreat.

I have a vivid and fond memory: I am eight years old. It is early, crisp and quiet. I pad up the hallway, through the kitchen and towards the deep cushioned armchair. The hours pass, my head bowed in my book. By mid-morning, bedsheets will be flung off and bedroom doors swung open. The house will become cluttered with conversation as my siblings and parents make a start on the day. But for now, as my eyes dash from line to line, the house feels enormous, the silence soft and spacious.

This habit has endured, despite having now lived for years with fewer people and in a series of larger rooms. I still seek out the quiet, crisp corners of the day. I move about the still house, or through the local grasslands, in the deep energy of silence. My mind feels vigorous from rest and wanders, unrushed and unlaboured by having to decode sound. It is in these moments that I feel like I can *think*, rather than react or recoil. But of course, this habit continues to be steadfast because it has a clear payoff – by nightfall my body feels flattened, my thoughts are tangled, after hours of the keen, relentless focus required to make sense of sound.

* * *

It took me until my late twenties to recognise how, or even when, I am fatiguing. It isn't heavy limbs and wide mouth yawning. It is a hard-edged sensation of effort. My body takes on the long list of symptoms of sensory overload: I become keen-eyed and riled up; relentlessly chatty even though my sentences become chipped or incomplete; restless and short-tempered, though completely indecisive; my heart thrums, too quickly, and I begin to feel streams of sweat running down my arms and legs. While I'm getting better at recognising this frenetic version of myself, I still need practice at herding myself home to rest.

When I enter a room, I do a quick, almost unconscious audit of the space. The walls and ceilings, the position of chairs and tables, the lighting and ambient soundscape. I look for exits, or places that I can walk quickly towards if I need to find relief, those moments of quiet and noiseless thinking. I spent most of my year twelve formal in the bathroom. At the time I didn't understand why my skin suddenly felt too small for my body, or my head so full and heavy; it just felt like I could exhale when there was a door and several walls separating me from the thump of 2005's top forty hits.

Now, when I can, I avoid places that trigger sensory overload. I make a list – cafes, bars, shopping centres, cinemas, stadium concerts, sporting events, protests, and city streets. The dull ordinariness of this list makes me realise that there are few buildings where I feel at ease, and just how narrow my world has become.

* * *

There is something about Churchill's argument about buildings and bodies that tugs at me. Not because I disagree with it, just the opposite, it makes absolute sense and this I realise, some months later, is the snag – his argument is flawed, even faintly ridiculous, but it makes sense to my body, a deaf body. Churchill appears to be passionately arguing for clear communication rather than the safeguarding of democracy. Historically, democracy flourished in a round, with large assemblies able to converge and to see one another. The actual design of the Commons Chamber is incredibly small and it is exclusionary even for elected members of parliament, as it contains only 427 seats for 646 MPs. Was Churchill concerned with his own body and how it would be shaped by the new Commons Chamber?

Churchill participated in the Commons Chamber debate in October 1944 and by December of that year his physician, Dr Charles Wilson, noted that the Prime Minister was having difficulty hearing on the telephone. Perhaps it is a coincidence. Perhaps Churchill's arguments for retaining a 'confrontational design' were motivated by wanting to retain the historical ties to British democracy, but all his reasons for the design benefit someone who is hard-of-hearing. I think of my own way of assessing spaces. The dread I feel when entering a wide-set room with high sweeping ceilings, where sound swooshes upwards and out of reach. The Commons Chamber is narrow, so that you can see the faces of your opposition only 'two sword lengths away', which is conveniently well suited for reading lips. Then there's the instant jealousy I feel when I read about the confrontational design, wishing that open-plan offices weren't so popular, that there would be more buildings designed for the exchange of ideas, instead of most buildings that make me feel misshaped.

Whether or not Churchill was motivated by his hearing loss isn't really the point, it is who and how buildings are designed that is relevant, and the fact that these decisions happen behind closed doors. These are conversations of power and with consequences, decisions that literally shape what happens to our society and our bodies.

The overlooking of disabled bodies is so consistent, so rampant worldwide, that the UN has created a checklist for politicians entitled: 'Why I should be interested in the rights of persons with disabilities'. It consists of six dot points, each a rallying cry of sense, which is not yet common enough to go unstated. The list begins with: 'The human rights of persons with disabilities should be promoted for the same reason that human rights are promoted for all other people: because of the inherent and equal dignity and worth of each human being.' The dot points are easy to scan as the language is plain and pointed. I bitterly laugh about the checklist with another disabled friend. We trade stories about how we cope. The ways in which we find ourselves backed into corners or avoiding, avoiding, avoiding the places that cause us to ache. Yet we know that this checklist is needed. As others, with able bodies, experience the world in seamless ways, entering and exiting buildings without friction or calculation. As parks and schools and workplaces and homes and even our Parliament House have been designed for their bodies. And so, I am the space where I am: orbiting the able world.

7

Dancing With My Telco

Joan Cahill

They could return my call
sometime in the future
so I wait the six promised minutes

agree to be recorded
and I want to say
and I am recording you too

dance a bit to the awful music
straighten two paintings in the living room
think about winding the clocks

but hands are in the way
put the singing on speaker
and flourish the duster

dance some more
How may I help you?
and sweet Nicole attends to Issue One

Issue Two
Stay on the line and I will transfer you
in youth we danced the Evening Two Step

to this music
no partner, not in a position to repeat this
so I sing along

just as well no partner
I wander outside phone in hand
examine some weeds

now I am bored
stand at the kitchen bench and read the newspaper
phone refrain and asylum seekers clash

a shiver of sadness at their plight
makes trivia of my cell phone challenge
and I contemplate hanging up

but Nathan appears from the ether
explains the steps to fix the problem
and the dance is over

in two elongated steps.

8

The Happy Family

Jeanne Viray

It used to be once a year that Dad would leave on a trip to go back home, but now it was happening every few months. With him gone, the house breathes.

My brother, Angelo, passed by the cabinet in our dining room one night. I had been brushing my teeth and he was throwing out a bag of chips he'd finished. Midnight. If Dad were here, he never would have allowed it.

'What do you want?' He had mumbled at the glass. 'Fuck you.'

Silence.

He stabbed his finger at the glass, breathing in a sob.

'*Fuck you.*'

* * *

When Angelo was seven, he would run around the floor of the Golden Palace and steal the porcelain chopsticks from the plates. He would stash the chopsticks under his leg when he sat down. He explained to me once that he always thought they were free, but he didn't want Mum and Dad seeing him take things like that.

Before moving out, we opened one of the boxes in his room and found ten pairs of high-quality chopsticks next to the socks he wore in primary school. Pristine white with holes at the toes and dirt at the heels. The first thing Mum said was: 'Why did you keep all these hidden all these years when we could've used them?' So, Dad took all of them and placed them carefully into the dishwasher, then put them in his cabinet.

When we moved, in the mess of everything, the chopsticks disappeared. Dad didn't seem to notice.

I think it's been a few months now, since we moved. Dad's been gone and back at least once. We've all breathed in and out. Tonight, we're eating fried noodles. Oil, string beans, pork, shrimp, baby corn. We're using forks.

Under the table, my brother is texting his friends. I look up in time to nod and smile as Mum looks to me for support.

'I'm okay with the house,' I smile wider.

'See?' Mum beams, sending the smile Dad's way. 'She's fine with it, everything's gonna be okay.'

The crease of Dad's brow deepens. Two moles on his head move with them. 'Yeah, sure, but... I still have to think about how we're going to make it work in here. How we're going to fit everything. All your things,' he points at me. 'All *your* things,' he points at Mum. 'It's a small house.'

'It's cosy,' Mum tries. 'Aren't you happy?'

Dad shakes his head, eating. His fork screeches against the porcelain of the plate. 'I'm fine, I'll work with it.'

Mum purses her lips.

Dad notices. 'No, no, it's okay,' he adds. 'Listen. It's fine, we don't need to talk about it. I'm happy as long as *you're* happy.' And, finally, he smiles. It is unsatisfying.

Mum reaches out to squeeze his hand. He goes to scoop himself up another serving of vegetables. Her hand falls into air.

I think of saying: *We'll work on it together, Dad.* But I don't.

'Have you started working on your cabinet?' Mum asks.

'Ah, I'll do that in my own time,' he answers, chewing a string bean. 'Don't worry about it.'

Dad's been telling us he'll do the cabinet in his own time since we bought it. It's *Fantastic Furniture*'s prodigal son. All glass windows. In happy times, he let us stack things in there like old cameras and DVDs we don't watch; and he threw Angelo's chopsticks in there. In bad periods, he'd throw everything out telling us he had nothing to himself anymore. His other excuse is that all his stuff is still overseas. Photos, awards, plaques. I didn't think we had left anything overseas. We always positioned our dining table in front of it. The cabinet, a tapestry to line the kingdom's achievements. His chair, the throne. We've moved three times for three different job-changes. Except in this new house, with no job, we had to set the dining table parallel to it.

It's a small house, so the throne room is gone.

I can see my reflection in the spotless glass, gnawing away at a string bean. I drop the bean on the plate when my fingers fumble. I just manage to hide my irritation at myself, but the glass catches it.

I frown.

'But, Dad,' Angelo says, glancing up from his phone, 'why is there something already inside?' We all look at him.

'Inside what?' Dad barks.

Angelo's eyes harden. 'The cabinet.'

'The what?' Mum arches an eyebrow at him. She softens. 'Angelo, please, don't look at your phone while we're –'

Dad pinches Angelo's arm under the table. I almost feel it.

'Put it away,' Dad warns.

'All right, all right –'

'Put it away,' I add.

'I'm *putting it away* –'

Mum puts her hand on Angelo's arm, an apology. 'What did you see?' She asks, forcing her voice to be even.

'I dunno, just something,' Angelo repeats, his phone now definitely away. 'Can't tell what it is.'

I pick up a single noodle with my fork. 'If it's just nothing, then don't talk about it.'

Dad shoots me a hard look.

He scolds Angelo for ten minutes about him not remembering *why* we were *where* we were, and is this what he brought us here for? To ignore our parents? Was he ungrateful?

Look at your sister, he said, *isn't she doing so well?*

* * *

Dad mutters to himself about the grime on the glass windows of the cabinet. None of us really see it, but he pulls me aside one day and explains:

Somehow it had gotten dirty in the moving truck. But I know it's because he puts his hand on it so often, listing all the things he wanted to show off. His hands have always been grimy, and if they're not grimy, they're filthy.

He'd meant to put a lot of things in there, he would say, but now he felt he couldn't. *Malas*, he'd say. Bad luck. *Malas talaga*. Always bad luck.

Another day, when I wake up earlier than everyone else, I clean the glass with surface wipes. I try out different faces in the reflection. There's still nothing in the cabinet yet so I see myself clearly.

The wiping motion makes the door shudder and there's a grunt from the couch.

'*What are you doing?*'

'Just cleaning. Sorry.'

Dad grunts again and falls silent. Mum snores softly from their bedroom.

I hold the glass doors down, so they don't shudder anymore, and I clean as quickly as possible. Dad asks me if I'm done yet. I look at myself in the reflection, tired.

The glass makes an ugly face back at me.

Dad asks me if I'm done yet.

'Huh? – I – *yes*.'

Sorry, the glass mouths at me.

'Sorry,' I quickly add.

Dad grunts his acknowledgement. I put away the rag and move out of the lounge, but I look back.

Mum is pointing out a spot in the glass that I missed and my reflection cleans it up. But I hear a snore from the bedroom.

* * *

Mum tells me that Dad's smoking again but not to mention it because he'll feel bad that he's been caught.

'He doesn't want you thinking any less of him,' she says.

'Maybe tell Angelo that.'

'I've told him that.'

'You don't need to tell me.'

She gives me a look. She was only meant to pass by my bedroom door, but now her hovering at the doorframe has her drifting towards my bed. Mum floats down to sit.

'What's wrong, honey?'

I'm sitting at my desk and when I roll my chair to the right, I can see the cabinet looking at me. I hesitate, getting up to close the door.

'He… wants me to find a framer, or something,' I speak slowly as I come back to her at my bed. 'Someone who can put all his hunting medals in a proper case.'

Mum smiles. A storm passes in her eyes and she looks like she's about to cry. 'That'd be wonderful.' She pulls me in for a hug and I smell the Pantene in her hair. 'You're such a good daughter, you know? You're such a big help for us, you have no idea.' She sighs. 'And you know what? You're going to be just fine. You're going to be wonderful.'

I sink into her hug. Behind her, my bedroom door has opened a crack and I see us in the cabinet glass. More handprints and dirt. I'm not sure where they came from, but I'll have to clean it up tomorrow.

* * *

Angelo has placed his chopsticks into the cabinet, tucked in a far corner. No one has noticed. Dad seems happier. I remember reading that you should watch out for people who seem suddenly happy after a period of serious depression. It could mean that they've found a solution to their problems. And we don't know what that solution is. I'd read this after typing in 'how to know if you're suicidal'.

But it's dinnertime soon, and we don't have time for that.

* * *

'How's your room look?'
We walk. 'Like this.' I show.
'Cool. And your brother's room?'
'He won't let us in there.'
'Huh. I would've just walked in.'
'It's a small house.'
'So I've heard.'
'How's your dad?' I ask.

'Fine. I guess.'

'Your mum?'

'Yeah, she looks okay.'

I wonder. 'Do you talk to your parents at all?'

'Yes?'

'But, I mean… how close are you to them?'

'Why, how close are *you*?'

'Never mind. Tell me what you see here.' We walk.

'The cabinet? It's empty.'

I frown. 'What, you don't see it?'

'What am I supposed to see? Finger-prints?'

'Wait, really? Shit, I just cleaned it.'

'It's not a big deal, don't worry. What am I supposed to see?'

'Me. It's me. I'm in there.'

'Yeah, nah, I'm in there too, it's the reflection.'

'No, no, I'm serious – it's like – I'm *in there*.'

* * *

Dad has finished an argument over the phone and he smells. He pulls me into a hug, his hands wide and gripping onto my spine.

'Ah, I love you,' he says.

I hug back. 'Love you too.'

* * *

I've emailed a framer and I've made Dad the casserole he likes, so he's happy tonight. I've assured him that he can eat as much as he wants; I've set aside half of the casserole for the rest of us.

I'm lying down as I pick up my phone. Check the time, check on the world. *He hugged me,* I think, *wiped those grimy hands on my back, and called me his favourite.* My phone falls from my hand and onto my face.

My face feels like it's shattered. Broken behind pious eyes. And there's a sound too.

Dad yells from the lounge. Mum tries to fix it. He tells her he can fix it better. She tells him she can do it. He tells her she can't.

My jaw hurts. My hands drag down my face again.

I remember my reflection saying that word.

Sorry.

I cleaned that glass so well. I found a framer. I cooked food.

And there's still so much to be done. But they tell me I'm wonderful.

My nails have been bitten down to the quick but I still feel them scratching at my eyes, pulling the skin of my face down like I don't want to exist. I don't want to exist.

I sink into the bed, and then through the covers, but I don't hit the floor. I don't hit anything. I sink. Just sink. No hugs.

* * *

The curtains of the kitchen window are drawn but there's a sliver of light that cuts through. It also cuts through my mother.

My brother notices it. I notice it. I've figured it out. The glass of the cabinet had become grimy again with more handprints. The light that reflects off it isn't as brilliant. Mum asks us if her hair looks dull and we say no, it looks fine. Mum asks Dad how her hair looks and he just shrugs and says it's fine. He turns to smile at me like it's an inside joke.

Mum blinks. Looks to the cabinet.

She goes to the kitchen and grabs the nearest rag. Opens the tap and splashes water all over it, and the kitchen bench. Before we know what she's going to do, she's slammed the rag onto the glass cabinet and started wiping. Cracking her hand on the window. I wince at every smack of fist on glass.

And we all know: *it's gonna break.*

* * *

There are two screaming women here tonight, and I see they are as different as night and day. The before and the after.

Screams of anger and screams of terror.

Maybe it's the scream that makes the glass finally shatter.

Then: blood on the rag. Blood on her hand. The red makes us *go*, instead of *stop*. Maybe there's a grimy hand behind me that pushes me forward, or a sharpened hand that pulls me in. But I want to stop her.

I rush to stop her from hitting the broken glass. Angelo's phone jumps out of his hand as he gets the first aid kit. Dad wraps his arms around Mum and I tell him to stop but I feel as if he'd killed me with the look in his eyes. *Follow.*

In the glass, my reflection is telling me to say: *Sorry.* Its eyes harden as if it's my fault.

* * *

Every glass door on that cabinet was destroyed except for the one I sit in front of.

'What do you want from me?' I ask.

My reflection stares. She points out the collar of my white shirt, it's creased and uncooperative. I pat it down.

'What is it?'

My reflection places her hands on the glass window.

'What do you want from me? They're coming soon, what am I supposed to say?'

She spreads her hands flat, patting the glass, gesturing for me to follow. I do.

'I'm supposed to tell them what happened, what do I do?'

My voice is strange. Warbled. I lift my hands and I can't push forward.

I push and the cabinet shakes around me. I hear Angelo's chopsticks roll around on the shelf above.

Get me out – get me out –

I'm screaming like her. Two screaming women here tonight.

I shove my hands forward. The cabinet convulses. These doors are latched but loose and I shake it so much that Angelo's chopsticks roll out one by one. He's not here – but see them. Pick them up. Please, pick them up. Do anything. See them. See me.

Dad comes over. He sees it sitting at my usual spot, and it's using my tears. He passes by me and places a dirt-stained hand on the glass. The dry, rough skin scratches against it.

He hugs the thing on the chair.

'I'm so sorry,' he says. 'I'm so sorry this has happened. But you're being so good, thank you. Thank you.'

9

Dwell

Alison Bernasconi

An ice cube falls and clinks into a small clear glass. Wider than the usual, and a good size for a good-sized hand. Another cube drops in and hits the first, splitting off a tiny spray of icy shards. Honey-coloured liquid splashes in and settles around the ice. The cubes morph into softer, smaller shapes.

I watch with satisfaction. I watch for too long as the cubes bleed into the whiskey. By the third glass it doesn't matter though. It's the first and second that matter. The taste wraps around the tongue. The slow unfreeze inside. The loosening of the mind.

'Don't romanticise the booze, Mum,' breaks into my reverie. I look over at Leah on the couch, crutches leaning against the wall. I scrunch my nose at her, and smile.

'Is dinner close?' she says. I look at the cooktop. Steam rising, a burning smell hits my nose, even with the extractor fan on. I jump up and wobble as I stand. I'm tired. My toe with the Morten's Neuroma hurts. I walk to the stove. The onions are sizzling brown and gone beyond the soft translucent pieces that are the beginnings of a good pasta sauce. Pale pink liquid drizzles down the side of the wooden board where whole and chopped tomatoes are piled.

'Are you drunk?' scoffs Leah.

'Not at all,' I scoff back, dribbling spit. I quickly wipe my mouth with the tea towel lying on my shoulder like a reptilian pet. I return to the table, pick up the whiskey and take it to the stove. The TV shouts at me.

'Do you know who the Minister for Women is …?' I don't hear the name of the person who the question is directed to. It sounds like *The Project*'s on. I recognise voices and tone. It's familiar. We basically see it every night of the week. Or should I say I hear it and Leah sees it. At least until her leg heals. I check the clock on the stove. Yeah. It must be *The Project*. Was it a woman or a man's voice? I don't know. I'm too caught up in my thoughts and cooking. I have another sip of whiskey.

'Could you turn it down please?' I say with a raised voice.

'Hey, do you know who the Minister for Women is Mum? Mum?' even louder the second time.

'No. Not tonight.' I can't do this tonight.

'What do you mean? You knew last night and tomorrow night, just not tonight?' Leah lets out a laugh, but it becomes a loud hiss. 'You are drunk.'

'Careful.' I take a breath. 'Actually, I think it's someone called Payne. Larissa? Marisa?'

'Is that a joke? Pain?'

'No. No joke. Not even funny,' I continue. 'Do you know what is funny and it's not actually funny either, is that Tony Abbot was the Minister for Women about six years ago. How the hell did that happen? I mean, really. That's just insulting.'

'Yeah. I was at school, it was ridiculous. He was Prime Minister. It's weird that Julie Bishop was like the only woman in the cabinet, and the Deputy Leader, and...'

'And Minister for Foreign Affairs.'

'Yeah, and he makes himself the Minister for Women's issues. Didn't he make himself the minister for something else lately?' Leah retorts. 'Indigenous Affairs?'

'Nooooo. You gotta be kidding. Maybe the CWA or gay liberals?'

'Ha.' We both laugh.

I return to making dinner as Leah turns back to the TV and her phone and her laptop. Someone is talking about skin cancer, melanomas, and there's a wallpaper of serious music and sad voices.

'Hey, did you know White Ribbon went into liquidation. How does that happen? That's like crucial for helping women, yeah, and families in domestic violence situations.' A pause. 'Oh my god, and Angie's the new Bachelorette.'

'Yeah. Rosie Batty will be devastated. Supports her life's work.' I say this more to myself.

As I finish chopping the last tomatoes on an already full board, I remember a postcard from the '70s of a woman grating something, like carrot, but she keeps going even after the carrot's finished and grates her hand up to her wrist onto an overfull plate. It was a black and white line drawing from a set of equally confronting pictures. It sat under a magnet with other postcards that said, 'the future is female,' and 'spilt guilt' featuring a woman crying over spilled liquid from a jug with the word 'guilt' in the spill and it was in a modernist dotty style, like Andy Warhol's Campbell's Soup picture, and 'Oh, I forgot to have a baby,' and another that said 'Oh no, I left the baby on the bus,' or something to that effect, on the old yellowing curved fridge in a share household, where milk crates saved our belongings and our lives.

I look at the postcards' contemporary relations on my fridge: magnets that say, 'Prepare your daughter for working life, give her less money than your son,' and 'I did not climb Ayers Rock,' and 'Extinction Rebellion,' and 'Oh no, I forgot to negatively gear,' and 'surely it must be five o'clock *somewhere,*' featuring a smiling blonde woman holding a full cocktail glass, and a local sparky's three point plug encouraging me to stay in touch.

The onions are crisp and curled and I stir them in a smear of oil, scraping the hardened bits from the base of the pan with the wooden spoon. I reach for the board where garlic and chilli are finely chopped, and I knife slide the small red and white piles onto the revived onions. The TV is crooning a '60s song, 'I love you baby, and if it's quite alright I need you, baby …'. It takes me back to primary school days and weekends with my family on the beach where hit parade songs were blasted out of big rusting speakers, and we rode foam boards, and body surfed, and surf life savers sprayed us with oil, and they had beach girl contests that I never entered, and we found glass coke bottles in the sand and got money for them.

'What's that advertising?' I ask over my shoulder. Leah doesn't answer. I turn around and she isn't on the couch and the crutches are gone. Still holding the wooden spoon like it's an extension of my hand, I walk around and look at the TV, but it's shifted to advertising rugby league with grabs of Roosters players getting tries. Grand final season.

'You should see this Snapchat. I can't believe she's doing this,' floats from Leah's bedroom.

'Can't hear,' I call back.

'Hey, Lizzo's coming to Sydney,' she shouts.

Thirty plus years younger, I'd be going to see Lizzo too. Impressive voice, good music, got a message.

I return to the stove and am relieved I'd thought to turn the gas down. There's a gentle sizzling mush developing in the pan. The juice from the tomatoes has spread from the board onto the stone counter creating a pink-ish puddle dangerously close to its edge. I juggle the board and slosh the tomatoes into the pan. I grab the fluffy yellow magic cloth from the sink and drop it on the puddle and watch as the cloth absorbs the liquid. Magic indeed. The near empty glass of whiskey sits to the side of the stove and I drain the last drop, sucking the reduced ice cubes. I half fill a big red pot with water and put it on the stove. I light the gas and put a lid on the pan with the sauce bubbling on the other jet. To the left, a small blue and white striped bowl is full of chopped parsley, a block of parmigiana sits on a crazed cream plate and green salad leaves lie twirled to the sides of a salad spinner.

With the empty glass in hand, I approach the chrome and Formica trolley, with its few bottles of spirits on the top shelf. But I hesitate and turn away and shake my head. In disapproval. Of myself. And stand in the middle of the room. TV blaring. Extractor fan churning out its monotonous tune. Feeling adrift. Tingles of shame spark inside my stomach and head.

I hit the off button on the TV remote control and with the relative quiet, realise my shoulders are practically up around my face. I walk back to the stove, turn down the extractor fan and check the water. Not yet boiling.

Strains of a piano tune float in the open kitchen window from the flats next door. The music pulls at me and I shut my eyes to hear it better. It fills me, and I know it well, as piano and bass and light cymbals and drums intertwine and blend and float melodies that open up a night in a different kitchen, where the smell of cooked leeks, spinach, eggs, fetta cheese and melted butter permeate a low-lit room, with lino floor and dirty cream rendered walls. A younger me, wearing a 'ban the bomb' t-shirt and Levis and bare feet, puts a tape in a cassette player and the Keith Jarrett Trio weave their magic. Iggy Pop, John Martyn, The Pretenders, Aretha Franklin and Marianne Faithful stand in line.

Alone and cooking for a couple of friends. My girlfriend and our house-mate are out. I know a few recipes, but my culinary skills come from looking in a fridge and making something from nothing. Music always accompanies, as does a joint. They are as much a part of a recipe as the ingredients. I am lit, happy and humming, chopping and cooking, as I layer the thin pastry leaves in the oven pan and paint on butter and pile on the spinach filling, and add the top layers of filo, slathering on more butter. Piled deliciously high in the pan, the pie goes in the oven.

My cocktail of happiness is fed by last night. Last night's dinner. A Greek restaurant, long tables, stools and benches, platters of dips and pastries and dolmades and shish kebabs and salads. A celebration for someone I don't know too well. Louise. She shares a house with another woman, Clarise. We'd all met out one night and liked each other immediately. Immediately.

Retsina, wine, beer and dragging on joints in a laneway behind the restaurant prime us all up, and when the Greek music comes on everyone jumps up, linking arms and hands and dancing in circles and shouting. I don't get up and neither does Clarise. We'd been talking, shouting over the table at each other, liking the repartee, making each other smile, sharing beers. No-one else in the room.

I move around beside her. Her smile, her wild curly hair, her hands, her laugh, her tight black clothes. Intoxicating. It's like there's another being inside her rippling to come out. I feel the pull toward her, the magnet of seduction, through her half smile, pale blue irises, and gentle reserve.

We talk to each other's eyes and mouths and scan each other's faces. When the dancers return to the tables we stay sitting together. Our knees occasionally bump under the low table and my awareness is pure nerves. Electricity is all I have. We talk less but I feel her more, filling my head and chest and belly, and my spirit leaves me and immerses itself in hers. I find myself talking to the man on the other side of me. I smile and nod and say 'yes' and 'no'. Auto pilot. Who am I? I don't know where my girlfriend is sitting. I only know I'm bewitched, gripped by something excruciating and captivating.

The waiter brings out an enormous cake decked with candles alit with excited flames and we all stand up and cheer. Clarise rises slowly and takes my hand in hers. I feel charged and light-headed. My smile hurts. I stumble as I stand. A rush starts low inside me and transforms to a feeling of nausea. She doesn't look at me, still holding my hand, but says into my ear, 'Hold on. Hold on, my dear'. And I think I will pass out. I think I will never be the same. I think, 'what am I to do with this?' And I stand there feeling fully exposed and yet invisible. She has me. I am hers. She has merged with my flesh and my heart and my brain and my blood.

Everyone sings, and I hear 'happy birthday'. To Louise. Who is standing with my girlfriend. Who looks at me with a frown. She pats her cheeks, lays her hands outward, and mouths 'ok?'. I nod and smile with cold closed lips. I feel pale. Everyone sits down, but I step back over the bench and walk outside. The darkness is profound after the light and energy inside. I sit on the kerb in the laneway and breathe slowly and wait until the nausea settles. I watch my hand tremble slightly and it doesn't belong to me. I feel like I don't belong to me.

I know what I want though, and I want her, to want me. And I think that is what is happening, and I believe what has happened is a form of truth, not to be denied, a shared mutual experience that has momentum and life.

I don't know that we start an erotically fuelled secret affair that takes me everywhere and nowhere. I don't know that she has male lovers, but she never said she wasn't straight. I don't know that intoxicants feed us, beyond each other. I don't know that her mother dies and her father dies a week later and how that can transform a person. I don't know that I don't know what I'm doing but am deeply convinced it is all I can do at the sacrifice of everything I have. I don't know I'm lost and can only feel found if someone wants me, needs me, desires me. I don't know that obsession is ritual that masks rejection, loss and grief. I don't know that it takes a long time to come to this, face this.

The hissing of water on the gas plate pulls me back into the kitchen like a meteor. I run the few metres to the stove and turn off the gas. I check the sauce. The jars of pasta are on top of the cupboards, so I walk down the hall to get the step ladder. On my way back, I tap on Leah's door.

'Dinner's up.'

'Ok. At last.'

'What's that mean?'

'Just that I'm hungry.'

'Well, pasta's on.'

I climb up the step ladder and grab the jar with linguine. I drop a big handful into the salted boiling water and return the jar to the top of the cupboards. As I fold up the ladder, I hear Leah return to the lounge chair, with the strike of the crutches' hard rubber tips.

'I mean, what have you been doing?' Leah says. I hear it, but I can't believe it. And yet I can.

'Sewing. What do you think?'

The TV is flicked on as I stir the pasta, and some police show is on. I vaguely recognise the theme music and the phrase 'heinous crimes'. American voices, and it sounds a bit gruesome. I make the salad, dress it with olive oil, balsamic vinegar and a pinch of salt. I watch the pasta in the cloudy bubbling water, and return to the heady, unsteady days where pasta never left the saucepan and bodies were al dente and salty.

'Sorry Mum.'

I turn around. Tea towel on shoulder, wooden spoon raised. Leah sits on the pale grey couch with its thick sides accommodating remote controls, water glass, novels and a sudoku book. Her leg is up on the foot stool.

'Can I have some ice please? And a cushion?' A very small voice.

'Of course.' My heart breaks as I fill an empty ice pack with ice cubes.

I continue. 'I'm sorry too. And I'm sorry you're out of action. It will get better. It is getting better. But it's not easy, is it?' I put the ice pack on her injured knee and a cushion under it.

'I don't want to talk about it.'

I go back to the kitchen. Fair enough. That's fair enough. I drain the pasta and combine it with the sauce. I grab a pair of tongs and serve piles of pasta into two bowls and top them off with parsley and cheese. An old metal tray sporting town and county sites from Grafton is loaded up with the bowls, salad, glasses of water, serviettes and cutlery. I place it on a small table beside Leah.

'Looks good. Thanks.' Leah picks up her fork. 'TV ok?'

'Whatever you want.'

And I stay in the room.

litany of gratitudes

Sue Goodall

the serrated edge labours
through a heel of kibbled rye
soft and moist a week ago

fridge and cupboard
yield skint offerings
a smirk of butter
a slur of marmalade
dregs of soured milk

pension day tomorrow

in this when-and-where
of waxing scarcity
I am paid to grow old

I have
this room on my own
eighteen floors
and a thousand stories above me
a roof keeps out the sky

I have
a kettle
a table

a chair quite like van Gogh's
a double bed
half slept-in

I have the power
in a single arthritic finger
to extinguish light
bring darkness to its knees
or interrupt a ruminating silence
with a string quartet
for one

I bask old bones
read poems
in my parcel of ruly sun
sip hot black tea, gnaw
sweet slates of buttered toast
sip tea
sip tea
sip tea

11

The Ruse

Callum Methven

I'm not really one to pray.

I mean it always seems a little silly for people like me because I don't believe that anyone is listening so instead of kneeling beside my bed in the dark with the television still on in the other room telling me what to buy, what I did was write a letter in blue ink with a pen I'd found on the side of the road on Hope street and paper torn from a book –

One of those soppy old romance novels my mum used to read with the two people about to kiss on the cover, you know the kind and well I hope she doesn't notice

– I wasn't entirely sure what to write or even how to address it (Mr Christ? Sir? To whose glory it may concern?) but I still had a lot of questions so I wrote them down instead in the hope that someone might answer them,

The very next day I went to the milk bar – not the one in Bunyip but down on the peninsula that's also a fish and chip shop in the afternoons but I don't like it then because of all the school children

And I bought a coke in a plastic bottle even though I wanted a glass one but I suppose a glass one might not float

I took a sip and tipped the rest down the drain and the gold and silver coins in my pocket rattled as if to tell me what a shameless waste it was, but what would they know about the comings and goings of a higher power (probably less than me) and anyway who were they to judge?

In the end I rolled the letter up and put it in the bottle and I screwed the lid back on tight

At the end of the jetty a man and a boy and a fish in a bucket said hello to me and asked me how my day was and to tell the truth I wasn't sure what to answer but luckily a lazy storm drifted in at that same moment,

I threw the bottle with the letter off into the water as a lone seagull sighed at the rain, so that the tide might take my message far away. I went straight home and I was in bed by six thirty without having said my prayers.

I slept in the next day because I wasn't particularly hungry anyway and I have a very effective set of red curtains drawn across the windows in my bedroom that my Nan gave to me one Christmas.

Later but not that much later as I scoffed back a bowl of wheat breeze-blocks I suddenly remembered the bottle and the message and the seagull whose day was ruined by the September storm

No sooner had the thought crossed my mind than I heard a knocking on the door

At the time I was listening to a Beatles double I'd found in the op-shop wondering whether or not I should get a haircut like George Harrison used to have back when Dad was a schoolboy so it's a wonder I heard anything at all.

You can only imagine my surprise when I opened the door to see not you, not me, but the fisherman from the pier standing there before me, a bucket in his hand!

My first thought was that my wallet had slipped from my pocket as I cast the bottle out to sea but there was a cheeky look in the bugger's eye and so of course I could tell that this was not the case.

Hello, I said to the man with the thin layer of white stubble frosted across his cheeks, are you God?

He didn't respond at first but to shake my hand and smile. I got your letter, said He, holding up the clear bottle with the red label, I hear you have some questions to ask.

'Holy shit!'

The words slipped out of my mouth before I could stop myself and without flinching I made the sign of the cross with my right hand, looked up to the sky for forgiveness from whomever was keeping the seat warm in his absence.

Obviously I invited the good Lord in and I put the kettle on to boil but he told me that he preferred Milo so I placed two cups of full cream milk in the microwave

I knew that is was not his real face for the Lord obviously looks a lot more like Morgan Freeman in real life but nonetheless I took a photograph on my phone of the two of us together and I sent it to my sister straight away knowing that she still wouldn't believe me

God sat down across from me

He put his feet up on the coffee table and he unfolded my letter smudged blue by a leak.

Alright, he said, ask away my child.

We were seven minutes and forty-one seconds into our conversation when he frowned at the lean on the coffee table and he took a hammer from his pocket that was obviously bigger on the inside which I thought was pretty cool

And as he was fixing it he explained to me that he too was a carpenter and an active one at that

But now that you mention it, I wondered aloud as he drove a nail through the upturned leg, I was just wondering how Jesus moved the boulder, I mean if there was a Jesus (is there a Jesus?) and why he bothered coming back and why he waited three days and if he had a favourite colour because mine is blue?

Ha! Why of course it was his very strong arms! He waited until night time when all of the disciples and all of the Romans were fast asleep and he moved the boulder with his firm, callused carpenter's hands.

He said it with a smile on his face but there was an echo in his voice that I've heard from absent fathers before

So tactfully I changed the topic and I asked him who wrote the Bible

He said that he didn't know but he seemed interested nonetheless,

But then why didn't they include any kangaroos or at least a wombat? Everybody likes wombats.

I like wombats too, but I'm sure there was something more important you had to say!

I rubbed my hands together and I thought long and hard about it: it's a little difficult to find the right words because, I said, there are so many of them they're like rabbits

When I was a boy I tried to read the bible once because I rather liked books and according to some people this was called The Good Book so of course I needed to know what happened in it before someone shared the ending at school

I sat down to read it and on the first page you created the Heavens and Earth and everything in the universe which I think is a metaphor because I can't even do more than one load of washing during the week

I asked the teacher about it and she told me that the universe was made in a Big Bang

It was a very long time ago (thirteen billion years ago, which is a 13 with nine zeros behind it) which is slightly longer than six days but that's not the point

As I kept reading I realised that there weren't any kangaroos in either Testament which didn't really bother me because I could see them down the road anyway, and besides I was more concerned about something else but see the bell went before I could ask the teacher,

I went straight home and I was in bed by 6:30 without having said my prayers.

God sipped on the hot chocolate malt drink with just a little bit too much sugar, with a glint in his eye that told me, *go on!*

Well I mumbled and so I continued on from there, if you created the entire universe before time, space and ideas had even bothered to exist and filled it up with planets and moons and stars and galaxies and superclusters and all the bits in between that you can't see because space is rather dark and Earth is just a pale blue dot from far away then I suppose that the human race is not the only one in this place that knows that it exists, so why oh *why* wasn't there anything about that in the Bible?!

The good Lord tipped his head back and he finished his Milo, and he kicked back, and it was good.

He cleared his throat and he shrugged again. I suppose, he said, that you humans must think you're a tad flash if you bothered to make yourselves the centre of the universe

Is that it?

That's it. I didn't come up with the ruse, I'm just the editor

He picked up his bucket and made his way over to the kitchen

And he placed the full bucket of fish in the freezer which was very kind of him because I wasn't having chicken nuggets for a third night in a row I mean I know my limits

And he walked to the door and I accompanied my guest and helped him into his jacket and I wished him a good day and he said he'd probably go fishing because it was a nice day for it and there's never a low tide on the bay down that way.

That night I prayed for the first time in a very long time,

And I have to admit it felt a little weird but I remembered something important that couldn't wait and so I asked Him:

Who the bloody hell wrote the Bible?

12

Third Rock from the Fire

JR Burgmann

Nightfall, a strange time.

Around the campfire the man and the girl draw circles in the dirt with sticks loosed from the branches of windfallen gums. Legions of tormented wood angels, thrown down, strewn across the great valley they'd wandered that day, heading for the coastline. Intimate and whorled lives upturned, their split innards showing their age in broken rings – broken seasons. The man accounted for some of the fallen giants, all far older and, in his estimation, far nobler than himself.

He is starting to forget their names – the ones people, in their endless race to collect everything, gave them centuries before. *Eucalyptus viminalis. Eucalyptus nitens. Eucalyptus Sieberi.* They have truer names, of course. The man has come, in time, to know that – feels its truth in the parts he holds now as he traces shapes in the earth with his only granddaughter.

He looks to her, beside him. She is swirling her branchlet, arm extended and making clear, decisive marks in the ground. A picture is forming. Of what exactly he cannot tell. As always, she does her own thing. Always will. He is merely partaking, dabbling. He tries not to cross her looping lines.

Focussing on her masterplan, her voice rises like a distant fog. 'What was this place, granddad?'

He considers this for a while, his furrowed brow clear by fire's light. 'A national park.'

'What's that?'

'A place.'

'What kind of place?'

This one's even harder. He looks to the stars for consolation and constellation. 'People used to come here. In great droves. In search of nature, or what they thought was nature... or something like that.'

'I see. But isn't that what we're doing now?'

'I guess so.'

She moves around the fire and, returning her stick to the earth, expands her oeuvre out into a wider space. She pulls her thickly woven cowl tight to her neck and begins, once again, to ask questions of her grandfather, all the while focussing on her work. How many she has asked in her life he cannot say. Thousands and more. Right from when she was very little, preparing for the world to come.

'Was it always so cold here?'

He almost laughs. 'You think this is cold?'

She looks directly at him for the first time tonight and nods. Her green eyes are devastating. He rarely gets to see them. Children look away from their elders now. *Planet eaters*, they each and all think. They are not wrong. The man sees this for the very inevitable thing that it is: take their world away – their air, their food, their safety – and they will turn away from you.

Her eyes, like the forgotten green of the oldest and most dense of rainforests, give him permission to continue.

'Used to be colder,' he explains, bracing his arms around his old, stiff body. 'Much colder, in fact. Winters here on the promontory, by the water.' He looks down toward the cove, dark and still but for flakes of moonglow shimmering on the seawater. He tries to remember the old shoreline. Where it began and where it ended in the shifting tide, before the first pulse. They are safe from high tide here, a meter above sea level – its rise humanly slow, geologically rapid. You could settle here for a night, but not a life.

The man looks back over his shoulder to the headland, the break he used to surf. He can just make out its shape in the night, pretend nothing had ever changed, filling the land with the details of old, wondrous memories. He would like her to see it as he does – as he did. He wishes the world had a better plan for her.

An intent little statue, she waits. She is not satisfied and wants more. He sighs before continuing. 'Cold fronts would come in all the way from Antarctica. Not the kinds of storms we have now. But icy winds that battered the coast here. Rain like bullets. Beautiful, now that I think about it.

Though back then we used to hide from that sort of thing, duck back into a tent or something. The weather felt extreme.'

'Antarctica? The ice place?'

He nods.

Content, the girl continues to make mysterious wrinkles in the dirt.

Whirling, the man focuses now on the gift he has for his granddaughter, stowed deep in the bottom of his pack, behind them by a charred stump of wood at the edge of the fire. A feeling like regret flickers through him. He suspects he's made an error but knows he cannot take it back. The gift must be dealt with.

'Come over here,' he says, inching nervously towards his pack. For just the second time tonight she looks up, wary beneath her hood, meeting his gaze. She circles slowly, stick in hand, around the dexter side of the fire to join him.

'I have something for you,' he says, trying to sound excited as he begins to rummage through his pack.

'What is it?'

He reaches right in and pulls out a fist-sized parcel wrapped in cloth, blotched with brown stains and damp with melted ice. He offers it to her, invites her to take it off his hands. She does so, drawing the parcel to her chest. She gags immediately, dropping it to the ground.

'What is that?!'

'Meat. For us.'

She does not hesitate. She raises her stick to his throat. 'Why would you bring that with you? You know what can follow us!'

He's ashamed. 'I know.'

'Is it real?'

'Yes. *Real* real.'

'What do you mean?'

'It's real meat. Not the lab-grown stuff. This type of meat, it's hard to get.' Illegal, actually, unless you are rich. 'We should eat it quick.'

'No, *you* should. It needs to disappear.'

The man kneels down to collect the fallen flesh. She gags again, though less viscerally this time. To the man's surprise his granddaughter begins to laugh. 'God that smells gross. I can't believe how much of this stuff you all used to eat.'

Her chirp is like no other sound in all his memory, a salve like honey that might keep him here on the earth a little longer.

'Me neither,' he agrees. 'But I wanted to share it with you. And then you can share with me what you've drawn.' He looks her over, remembering how fat kids and teenagers used to be. He slowly encircles a free hand around her upper arm. 'You are all so skinny these days.'

She pulls away. 'I'm fine.'

'I know you are.' He unwraps the cloth, the dank musk of meat wafting between them, and says, 'If you don't want any, I understand. But I don't know if I can eat all this by myself.'

'You'll have to.'

He raises his eyebrows, looks down to consider the strange lump in his palms. 'I don't know if I can.'

She moves closer to him and slips both her arms around one of his. She leans against his shoulder, looking at the gift. 'Eat what you can and if you can't finish it...'

'...What?'

'Let's just see. But we need to get rid of it.'

'I know. I just want it gone,' he says, remorseful.

'You're an old fool.'

'True.'

Later, as the meat bursts and hisses, hanging there over the fire from what was his drawing stick – an article imbued with great powers of creation – the old man wonders if he can remember how to cook the stuff. But even after all these years it comes to him. Satisfied at the browning, he brings it down into his lap and slices through it. It awakens something wonderful and awful inside him. He devours it. Forgets everything. When he finally looks up, juice dripping from his chin, he sees his granddaughter, perched on a log, knees drawn up to her chin in utter fascination. 'That. Was. So disgusting.'

'Were you just watching me this whole time?'

'Bit hard not to.'

'I'm sorry. But I'm glad you didn't have any.'

'Clearly.' She leaps down and returns to her drawing, her masterplan. 'I probably would have had some, you know.'

'I'm glad you didn't. Your mother would have killed me.'

'She wouldn't have needed to find out.' He hears the threat but is too full to care. 'Now, may I see what you've been drawing?'

'I'm not quite finished.'

'Is any artist ever?'

'Yes. Me. I finish things.' She moves back and forth across the site, making great arcs and violent dissections, bifurcating elaborately both nearby and far from the centre, where the fire, tended to every so often by her grandfather, pops and crackles. She goes about her business and he pretends to go about his, until she finally approaches him. She takes him by the hand and drags him through the dark up to the top of the small dune system, eroded beyond recovery, overlooking their camp. From a vantage of just a few metres the picture takes on a whole new life, lines forming into great cosmological meanings. Our solar system, there in the sand and soil.

The fire is the sun. The many small circles she swirled, the planets. The great ellipses she lassoed around the fire, their orbits. Between the orbits of what he thinks must be Mars and Jupiter, a frenzied ring of blemishes makes a great asteroid belt. And there, third rock from the fire, ludicrously expanded to allow for great detail, is our Earth. It moves him. He manages eventually to ask her if this is something she learned in school, back in the city; she explains that she learns nothing at school.

She then leads him back down, dragging him across the hazy band of stars into this quadrant of our galaxy so he can see it anew, up close. He takes in the oversized Earth, its continents and oceans all squished and rendered artfully in two dimensions. He does not bother to ask what is on the other side. A dozen or so dots mark cities. Berlin. New Amsterdam. Buenos Aires. Miami Pontoon. London. Toronto. Beijing. The rest he's not so sure of.

'I love it! What does it all mean?'

'Well, nothing really.'

'That's not true.' He shakes his head in wonder. 'Why these dots? These cities?'

'They are the places I'm going to go.'

He moves over to her, wraps his arms around her while he still can. The touch ties him to a memory of when she was only very little. It's faint but true. Of her drawing something similar – stars and suns – in yellow and blue crayon on genuine paper sourced from a tree. She always giggled when he rolled out those old sheets for her to draw on. *Feels funny*, she would say, scratching her tiny fingernails along it.

He turns to her now, anxious. 'Why do you want to go out into the world?'

'Because I'm going to help it,' she says, fierce and certain in a way he could never know.

13

Pushkin's Saint

Yanping Gao

And they walked, many a time, over the goose's grave,
'Did you hear the birds talking?'
Tilt your ears, you asked.
Only that time she did not forget.

The purple of Jacaranda falls, and the robin returns to the grave.
The footprints grow again and go again.
Pushkin's saint is in Moscow,
Winter snow sent from St. Petersburg, the remnants left on the
    letter like tears.
She is watching monitor lizards in Komodo.
A five-year-old boy fell under their paws.

The second farewell was in the summer,
Then,
Her tears fell as sudden as summer rain.
Pushkin's saint wet his temples,
His nose had disappeared,
'London Caesar's nose fell off in the same way.'
They said as the lights were turned off in the British Museum.

Natalia comes, and she strokes her chin,
Look up,
'A duel is the only way to get the saint.'

The little trees grew up around the goose's grave,
She walked back and forwards,
for the last time,
Pushkin's saint returned to Moscow,
Forever.

14

Our Memory

Michael Walton

Today, I received an invitation from the Bell Foundation to speak at a memorial service on the seventh of September. I was asked for a written contribution as well. They were sponsoring a volume of essays in Bell's honour. They wanted me to write both personally and professionally, reflecting on the impact of Bell's work over the past fifty years.

So. It has been fifty years already.

Alex Bell, better known as the Golden Bell, was an essayist, activist and social revolutionary, often credited with the abolition of binary, hierarchical gender. They were a key figure in the early Red-Pill Revolution and have been described by Professor Michel Weathersted as 'the most influential writer of the twenty-first century'. Alex Bell, the tragic victim of a hate crime, died on the seventh of September.

That is the biography of Bell on the Foundation's website. They've misquoted me. Taken my work of out context. Removed the parts where I speak of the other victims of gender-based violence and name those responsible. I suppose that was to be expected.

I am a Professor and therefore an authority. I am asked for opinions I am not qualified to give; then that opinion is taken as truth. I am misquoted alongside my idol; the both of us have been cast into sacred offices by virtue of our apparent insight.

We make the insensible universe sensible for an audience or, more often, provide the slightest appearance of sense which the audience seizes onto. Neither Alex nor I claim to speak with authority, we rebel at the very idea of it; but by the act of writing down our thoughts, or by speaking on stage, we are claiming it anyway. Authority, it seems, is inescapable. Like God, but on a smaller scale.

I take up my pen.

* * *

To the Bell Foundation,
R.E. The Death of Alex Bell

Once, I might have told you about the possibility of meeting Alex in the next life; or the fruits of paradise with which they were to be rewarded. I might have spoken of the widows of Melbourne wailing on September seventh. I might have said that I tore my clothes and my hair that day, beating my breast until it was purple with bruises.

All these things I might have said. Then I would have loaded our collective guilt and grief onto the backs of the gods and then banished them with soothing platitudes. But then the gods died; and we are left to the business of mourning without them. How does one mourn in a secular age? I have no answers. Only questions.

When Alex died, I was still young. Young enough to ride on my father's shoulders and look out across a sea of shifting people who had gathered at City Hall on the eighth of September. There was the most profound silence that day; save for the shifting of clothes, the shuffle of feet and the impatience of children. The traffic stopped to observe our grief.

We stood for hours, my father bearing me on broad shoulders, as people came and went. I watched them pay homage to a photo someone had framed. Flowers. Photographs. Clothing. Candles. Essays. Stones. On the pavement, someone had written:

In lieu of flowers
    bring us change
        it will not fade so fast

    There were police there in bright yellow vests, a dozen or more at every street corner. They tucked their hands into their vests; concealed their impatience by scrunching their toes in black boots. I did not need to be grown to feel the power of the crowd; so solemn and listless in their movements. Some part of my mind, inherited from my ancestors, recognised the anger which lay iridescent just beneath their skin. How that fire would burn in the days to come, I could not have known.
    Flowers and fury: that's how Alex Bell was remembered.

Regards,
Prof. Michel Weathersted

* * *

I sent that manuscript to the return address on the invitation. It is not what they wanted. They wanted to know how I could have devoted my life to studying Bell; when the divine spark leapt from Bell's writings to me, bestowing on me the skill as a writer with which I have lived. They wanted to see how my life was wrapped around Alex's and then shake their heads and say: 'I could never be a disciple like that. I could never devote myself to so completely to anyone.'

No doubt spouses would smack their arms in jest for that. I feel that I ought to light a candle before I take up my pen again.

So. I do.

* * *

To the Bell Foundation,
R.E. *Life & Times of Alex Bell*

The use of the Red Pill, the drug which allows for fined-tuned control over one's secondary sexual characteristics, was once the most divisive political issue in Australia. The deregulation of this pill, and its subsequent commercial availability, catalysed the abolition of hierarchical, binary, gender. But change does not happen overnight. For a decade or more the pill was bitterly contested with various political groups seeking social and legal controls over its use.

One of those was the infamous article 21. This forbade the teaching of Red Pill Positivity (RPP) in government funded schools. It banned RPP books, music and films, and 'concerned citizens' tried to use it to close libraries which refused to comply with these standards.

Fortunately, the law of supply and demand mandates that all the morals in the world will not stop a product that people are willing to pay for. RPP culture thrived on the attempt to squeeze it out of existence; there is no surer way to encourage people to read something than to ban it.

Prior to the passing of article 21, Bell was the host of a moderately popular talk show, *Bells and Whistles*, and wrote the occasional essay. Though they were renowned for their razor wit and acid pen, it wasn't until they published the seminal essay 'Taking Your Medicine: A Defence of the Red Pill' that they were finally heard. Once you have heard Bell ring, you can never forget them.

After that, the Golden Bell began a long and public campaign against article 21. They were everything an essayist should be; infuriating, brilliant, highly provocative, and, above all, never silent. I wonder sometimes on the toll that this must have taken on Alex; what skin had they shed in order fight like that?

They were never afraid of an argument and answered all serious objections to their writings, revising their finer points a number of times. Invariably, the magnetic appeal of their writing

and their mastery of rhetoric produced works in which every
sentence rang true. As the Red Pill debate intensified, politicians
rushed to pledge their support on one side or the other. Parliament
was split down its centre.

Bell was not the first to attack article 21 but the clarity and
wit of their writing, matched with their public persona, made a
devastating combination. Bell was the first public figure to come
out as a user of the Red Pill and they did so as the first speaker
in a national debate on the issue. They took the Pill in front of
an audience, which loved and hated them in equal measure, and
began their speech with a bow.

As they spoke their body changed. Pill users were often the
target of cartoons, mockery and caricature, but there was no
humour in Alex's eyes. For once, the glamour was lowered. The
audience saw Alex without their armour; a dragon whose scales
had fallen away.

In that moment Alex was naked. As they spoke, their voice
cracked stumbling to a stop. But they recovered with grace.
Like an actor who misses a line, only to recover their place in a
moment. It was in that moment, that Alex Bell's words entrenched
themselves in the heart of the audience. It was then that the
heathen threw down their idols and flocked to the altar.

The Golden Bell became the image of their age; the figure
around which many RP users rallied to fight for recognition and
acceptance. Even I, small as I was, could see that the tide had
turned. So: at the failure of debate and words, the enemy turned
to violence.

That was the last public appearance that Alex Bell ever made.

The seventh of September was a crisp spring morning. Alex
Bell was on their way to their place of work; a Fitzroy café called
The Wicked Sister. They never made it. There is a photograph,
taken from a street camera, of Bell the moment before it
happened. In the background of the image, between the shadows
and the grains of the photo, there are three shadows: blurred and
indistinct.

And so it goes.

On the eighth of September, a newspaper ran with the headline 'For Whom the Bell Tolls'. There was a smugness amongst more conservative commentators, many of whom had been the recipients of Bell's blistering pen, and a sense that Bell had got what they deserved. Many simply shrugged their shoulders; 'they shouldn't have been walking alone.'

Today, we condemn these people and, in doing so, condemn part of our own history. This is a folly; no matter how appealing it is. You have taken up the position of victor and writer; authoring a history which positions Bell as a tragic hero and their opponents as tyrants and fools.

I witnessed the first inscription that day at City Hall.

Regards,
Prof. Michel Weathersted

* * *

Two-thirds of my duty is done. All that remains is to speak. The day before I was due to address the Foundation I drove to The Wicked Sister in Fitzroy. Once, this might have been called a pilgrimage; I might have been blessed before I departed and offered food and shelter along the way. I might have arrived in the Holy Land dusty and travel sore. I might have accomplished something when I arrived.

Now, my old knees protest as I shuffle over the bluestone gutters. I cross the threshold and sit in a stiff wooden seat. My reflection examines me from the polished table surface.

Alex is all around me: in the headlines of yellowing newspapers, in framed photographs and in the signed pages of essays, torn from their context to be displayed as trophies on the walls.

In Rome, when a general wore the garment of Jupiter in triumph, a charioteer would stand behind them and whisper in their ear: *MEMENTO MORI*. Remember death. But the stables are empty, and all charioteers, gone. The menu is overflowing with bell-related puns: *a chocolate ring, the silver clapper* and all the rest. I feel compelled to compliment the owner on their marketing strategy. Death, it seems, is a rather profitable business.

Was this their way of remembering Alex? Have we replaced statues and sanctums with discounts and value meals? Is that what it means to be immortal now?

Alex had sat here, writing a new world into existence; one which has radically shaped my own. The thought passes my mind, but it has no impact. Whatever it is that pilgrims seek, it is not here. I look down at myself; at my shawl, my boots and my scarf. I wonder what the world would have been like if I had been forced to wear a suit for the rest of my life, because, when I was born, a doctor peeped between my legs and said: 'It's a boy!'

* * *

I am driven from the Sister in search of Alex. An array of people saunter by me in regal silks, fake furs and dark jackets with boots that clop and click against the stones. Some are happy. Some are sad. Most are indifferent. There are no men or women. There are only people.

Is this where Alex is to be found? Among those who benefit from them? Those who live their lives by the rhythms and rituals Bell authorised? If I were looking for Jesus, that's where I might find him.

But Alex? Maybe not. Perhaps they are on that street corner or that stage, where they are forever caught in frozen light. Perhaps they are in that shallow grave where the body was dumped. Or maybe Alex is in their mashed face and broken ribs; identifiable only by their teeth.

Maybe Alex is everywhere and nowhere; is it the act of visiting a site that makes it holy? I shuffle on down the street and try to avoid inconveniencing any of the people who rush by me; propelled by tides I long ago renounced.

'Weathersted is a national treasure,' said the reviewer of my last collection of essays, 'a beacon for the ages. The most powerful essayist since Bell.' It was a nice review. I think I am more like the national equivalent of one's Sunday best; only shown off at special occasions and even then, only briefly. They wheel me out for this ceremony or that and people applaud politely as my voice cracks and wheezes its way to the end of my speech.

The audience lean their heads together and says: 'Have you read their latest book? No? Me neither.' Then they go back to applauding. I am a garment for special occasions. Alex is for all seasons; the kind of writer who, in dying young, will live forever.

* * *

In the mirror, I see an iron-haired writer, far past their prime, trying to seem relevant. I see a child staring into the eyes of Alex Bell, unable to hold them because their father is swaying beneath them. I see evenings spent in communion with Bell's words; making them into sacred ground for the generations to come.

I take the stage on the seventh of September, the same stage on which Alex Bell had walked the day before they died. I peer down my multi-focal lenses, trying to bring my script into focus. I clear my throat, lean into the microphone, and hear my own breathing like a hurricane. If they had wanted a better performance, they should have hired an actor, not a writer.

I read slowly and clearly: making up the bits that I couldn't quite see because of the stage glare. I speak of a time before Bell. I speak of gender-based violence, knowing only the old-folks would remember it. I speak knowing that the young have already condemned such behaviour unequivocally. 'Can you imagine that?' They say. 'A world where your genitals determine what kind of life you can live? What kind of violence you would be subjected to?'

I want to shout at them; to shake them until their teeth rattle. Scream until understanding flows from me to them. This was within my lifetime; your parents and grandparents were perpetrators. Show some shame for the blood that runs in your veins!

I watched as the city came together to mourn Alex Bell and I understood, even as a child, that it was not just Alex that they were mourning. They were mourning for siblings and parents, for friends and family who had been kicked to death in alleys by thugs who went home to eat dinner afterwards. As a nation, we remember the one and assume it will stand in for the many. Then, the nation forgets the many.

I am shouting now, and audience is shifting. They will never invite me back; they are wishing they hadn't invited me. I do not care for the breaks in my voice or the wheeze of my failing lungs. I speak. I speak and know I will be mocked, ridiculed and scorned for it. I speak because the outrage and the shame overwhelm all my powers of calculation so that I have no choice but to act. I have no choice but to speak.

I look up from the podium and my eyes fall on a watercolour of Bell, in the garb of Jupiter, holding winged Victory in their hand. The portrait looks nothing like Alex really did. The artist has removed the asymmetry in their face, cleaned up their spots and made Bell smile more warmly then they ever did in life.

'Memento Mori Alex Bell,' I wanted to say, but they are beyond death now. I pause and push the tip of my tongue against my teeth and prepare to articulate the Latin with which I conclude.

'*Si monumentum requiris circumspice*,' I said, exhausted at last. My eyes remain on Bell's, 'if you would seek my monument, look around you.'

The applause is half-hearted.

* * *

Afterwards, I decline the invitation to dinner, pleading my health. I suspect the other guests breathe a sigh of private relief. 'What business did they have bringing up such unpleasantness?' They will say. 'Don't they know that times have changed?' On that, I must concede. Times have changed. It seems that change is not a process of growing after all but a ritual of forgetting; a selective memory.

I drive to Fitzroy and park in an alley. I shuffled to the Sister and take a seat beside the window. There is coffee on the table. Alex Bell sits across from me, watching with tiger eyes.

'You will stand forever in the memory of this nation,' I say, 'You, the god. I, your priest. We, the anarchists, have become the institution.'

My eyes close; I am too old for the irony.

'We will be cast into roles that suit their story. Our names will grace the pages of nationhood, to be used however they please. Our words with authorise a history we did not endorse. It will be canonised; become truth. Then, at last, the business of nation building can move on.'

Alex Bell takes my hand. We sit as writer and reader in certain knowledge that we have become nothing but fictions. We sit; waiting for the eighth of September.

15

The Number was Hers

Rebecca Bryson

The summer was as hot as it could have been, as his footprints sunk into the softened black tar of the road. Hot and sticky, it was molasses under foot, while the magpies cawed lazily above. He was on his own now, with a prickly red pube-stubble chin where he'd shaved two days prior. One day on, one day off. His hot-coloured strands of beard betrayed him by worming their way out of his chin, reminding him that the days are stubbornly passing.

A van roared around the corner, nearly clipping his foot as it came to an abrupt stop. His foot stayed suspended above the ground, his skin prickled despite the heat. And his face. His face was drawn and white in the curvy reflection of the van window. Waning and draining, his blood in his heart. Dusty and husky, the van sighed and relaxed onto its haunches, waiting for the traffic to clear.

John Crandle Plumbing Solutions.

And then a number. It was one that he knew. It was exactly hers. She had written it on the palm of her hand in a leaky black marker and pressed it to his. He unjumbled those backwards, upside down numbers that night, drunkenly focussing on the crooked nine and the maimed seven. The act of unfurling the precious digits had made him remember by heart. She was in his phone, still, with her name and a heart and a smiling emoji. Who could delete her?

He couldn't. He just couldn't. His heart again. Jumping and thumping. But of course, she was gone, as of the year before last. On a day just as hot. She'd been wearing her stark white ear buds, stuffed perfectly into her ears. Noise-cancelling, was what she had wanted. To block out the sadness of train carriage ramblings, the wailing on the street and the under-breath cursing. It was frightening, she said. They'd told him that she'd been listening to an audio book as she crossed the street, as she crossed the white-hot tram tracks. He tried to imagine the distracted thoughts in her mind as she hurried, too engrossed to check for trams. She thought about making pasta for dinner that night, and she thought she'd make salad. She thought about how she loved him, and she thought about how maybe she didn't. And then her number, he never thought, would be anyone else's number. Returned to the pool of jumbled digits when her father had scanned and emailed her death certificate to the phone company. Returned to the pool and fished out again, by John Crandle. Plumbing Solutions. The first thing about her he had learnt by heart, meticulously reconstructed from the smeared and faded imprint, was etched on the side of a dirty van. It stood stark and obvious, in a plain stiff font that wasn't jumbled at all. No unfurling was needed, no excitement in discovering that it had been correctly deciphered. No mystery that had made his heart gambol, the sound of his own text message tone sending a pleasurable tingle running through his veins. The sight of that number illuminating his phone screen, glowing and promising. But not now. No thought behind the first text, no analysing each emoji and punctuation mark.

It was just… John Crandle.

Plumbing Solutions.

A woman glanced at him, mildly interested in the way that he faltered while crossing the road, weaving carefully around the van that had stopped in the street. Everything was normal.

How could anything look out of place? How could anyone know that his heart had just been cracked, like the shiny screen of a phone, all over again.

16

Lucky Charm

Olivia Shenken

One day in December, Archibald Truck drove out to Warrnambool so he wouldn't have to spend the summer in the same city as his students. Before he left, while he was clawing his way out from under geological formations of Term Four reports, he couldn't stop repeating to himself the same thought, just as an adolescent boy rewinds the dirty scenes on a VHS:

Woe be to education students. Woe be to them. Woe be to education students. Woe be to them...

Thinned-out, worn, damaged, like overused film. That was Archibald. Nonetheless, he kept thinking it. Couldn't stop.

For the whole drive to Warrnambool, Archibald switched the radio station whenever a youthful voice came on. Eventually he settled on the most monotone talk station he could find, the kind where the host invites experts to speak about the intricacies of cloud identification. He would have stayed tuned, except the wistful presenter began to recall an afternoon spent making up stories about cloudshapes with her young sons...

For the remainder of the journey, Archibald drove in silence.

* * *

Because he was a secondary school teacher, the only holiday Archibald Truck could really afford was in Warrnambool. This was not because he had very little money – certainly not enough to afford a trip to a more desirable, expensive location, with nicer accommodation. It was because he had no money, and was receiving free accommodation from his parents.

He had left the place seven years ago with a smile plastered on his face, spry and youthful and bright, ready as anything to go off to university in the big city. He had not expected that his first years teaching would leave him so desolate, so sucked dry of life, paper-thin and brittle-skinned. That every sight and sound that had become familiar to him in Melbourne would clang with reminders of his classroom humiliations, of the workload that had given him palpitations. He had never thought that Warrnambool would be a balm.

Nor was it. It didn't hold much for him that he lacked or missed. No, the real reason was that it was not Melbourne. That was all. Warrnambool was not the setting of his failed stint as a teacher. And he was unlikely to bump into any of his old students here, or so he hoped.

Once he arrived, he sought out his old haunts, and began to lose the twisted edge in his voice, the crick in his neck, and the twitch in his eye. His symptoms only relapsed when his career was brought up in conversation by the unwary, or when he slipped and chanced to spare a thought about his future.

His mother quickly learnt which topics to avoid around Rick, as she called him. Schools, teachers, any of Archibald's old friends from uni. And, of course, his work. The hardest thing for her was that any mention of children would visibly tighten Archibald's jaw. For this reason, Linda Truck postponed announcing the pregnancy of her daughter Catherine to anyone at all, let alone Archibald, until three weeks after she had received the phone call from Brisbane.

One Tuesday afternoon, the two of them sat down for lunch at the kitchen table, the blinds drawn against the midday sun. Archibald was assembling a sandwich while Linda considered the newspaper crossword. They sat in companionable silence. Once each little blank square housed its destined letter, Linda looked up at her son. He felt the gaze.

'You know, Rick,' Linda said, her voice hesitant, 'I'm glad to have you here, and – and to see you're getting out of the house so much.'

Archibald nodded.

'It's good to get some sun,' Linda went on, starting to nod herself. 'When you arrived, you looked as if you'd been cooped up inside all year, reading.'

Archibald smiled at that. He *had* been getting out lately. He knew a nice shady spot, out of the way and far from nosy parkers, that was perfect for lazing around with a good book. Just that morning he had flown with the dragon-riders of the planet Pern, and the day after he planned to rediscover the spaceship Rama with the crew of the *Endeavor*.

Linda turned back to her newspaper while Archibald put the finishing touches on his sandwich. He was just reaching for the teapot when his mother struck again.

'Rick – do you still write your stories? I'd love to see some.'

Archibald made the sensible choice of gently lowering the fragile teapot back onto its tray.

'No, Mum. Not really.'

'Oh. Well, that's understandable. You must've been so busy with… things.'

Archibald nodded a pathetic, limp nod. The corners of his mouth were actually pointing to the floor. He was afraid he was going to weep.

Linda got up, gave him a kiss on the cheek and prudently hurried out of the kitchen. As she left she called back:

'Well, anyway, if you want to pick it up again, Catherine's old type-writer is still here!'

Archibald put his head in his hands and whimpered.

* * *

It was a mortal summer, with an end in sight, and eventually all the possibilities that entailed began to lighten Archibald's spirits. He grew strong enough to briefly consider his work-related crisis. Only briefly, though.

It was in this period of recovery that his mother informed him of his prospective unclehood. By then, the taunts of children had faded just enough in his memory that Archibald could wholeheartedly revel in the good news. He had never been a big drinker, but he got slowly and pleasantly sloshed with his father as they sat on the veranda that night, celebrating.

Catherine's typewriter had been on his mind as much as her burgeoning family. Archibald entertained the idea of typing up a letter of resignation. But he didn't see much use in it, in the end. He handwrote a few letters to some of the more memorable students – never sent, of course – as a therapeutic exercise.

But after the ink was dry, holding those letters in his hands, Archibald felt small and mean-spirited. A persistent voice in his head whispered that he was imitating the immaturity of his students.

He burnt the letters.

He had *wanted* to be a teacher – why was that? He asked himself that question the next morning. All through the rest of the day he repressed the thought, but in a quiet moment as he read underneath his tree, he acquiesced and let it ring its clear chime.

Why? Because he loved to teach. He had thought he would work best with teenagers. He didn't know if that was true any longer, but it had been once.

'The only way,' he said to himself, quietly, under the shade of his reading tree, 'is to keep teaching. Only way to find out.' He sat on that for a minute or two. 'Maybe this is just a bump in the road.'

He found the thought of picking up his book again unpleasant, and yet remaining in the tree's shade to ponder was equally so. Getting to his feet, he hugged the paperback to his chest and headed back towards the road. Archibald usually dawdled his way back to the house from here, but that day his path was as straight as the crow's. Something propelled him – he knew not what. All he knew was that he was in a hurry to get home.

When the front door came into his line of sight, Archibald quickened his step. His breath caught in his throat and his hands shook as he slotted the key in the lock, turned the knob, opened the door, burst into the corridor...

...He had forgotten. The thought had been right there. And walking through the doorway had extinguished it. He tossed his head around wildly, desperate for a clue, a sign, an epiphany. His eyes lit upon the door to his room. Bingo.

He pushed his bedroom door open gingerly. On his desk was Catherine's typewriter, where it had been sitting, unused, for weeks. He stepped further into the room, pulled out his chair, and sat down.

Archibald stared at the typewriter. Every time he had considered writing a story, he had fastened the thought away at the back of his mind, chained and shackled the desire. The typewriter had taken on a sinister aura, and if he woke up facing his desk in the morning he would turn the other way and wallow a while before getting up.

Here, now, sitting before the heavy thing, it seemed a silly fear. All he had to do was write. Just lift his finger to the keys, and type.

He sat for twenty-five minutes, staring, then glaring, at the typewriter. He was awoken from his reverie by the slamming of a door in a neighbour's house. Abruptly he slid the desk–chair back and left the room, left the house.

* * *

He wandered. It was a hot day, and he soon wished he wasn't out in the sun but was rather at home with a nice fan by his side. He might have gone into any shop, but right as he was getting a little sweaty, he thought that he would rather like to see the Warrnambool Antique Market. Just to peruse, to browse. Maybe find a pretty, cheap little trinket that would raise his spirits.

As soon as the thought occurred to him, it ballooned. Archibald made his way to the market and stood on the pavement, staring into the open doorway and imagining in great detail how he would wander casually through the aisles, until his eyes were drawn with magnetic inevitability to the exact object. A talisman.

'A talisman,' he breathed.

An old man sitting on a nearby bench raised his head, which had been resting on the top of his cane, and looked up. 'Did you say something, son?'

'No, sorry.' With a hurried step, he entered the Antique Market.

It was pleasant to be out of the heat, but Archibald's spirits only plunged as he shuffled through the large building that housed the market, edging around tables and shelves and trying not to knock anything over. No talisman could solve his problems. Although there were many marvellous and intricate artefacts on show, Archibald was not innocent enough for such wonders to awe him. There was always a corner of his psyche that nagged at him. Sometimes, it was enough that he wanted to die.

He stayed there a long time, longer than he had intended to. Something would catch his eye, and he would consider buying it. But if he began crowding his room with useless knick-knacks he would only get angry with himself.

There were porcelain cats, glass sparrows, a surprisingly cheap landscape painting which was nevertheless over his budget, a functioning barber's pole, an owl-shaped clock. He knew he ought to just leave, but he had nothing more engaging to do at home. This thought did not alleviate his depression.

And then there was the dog statue. The first time he noticed it, he looked at it a moment, smiled, and continued on his rounds of the market. A few minutes later he returned and considered it a little more closely. It was a pretty thing, and pretty cheap, too. A little shorter than the length of his hand, the reclining dog's blue-black surface was painted over with geometric patterns in green, sky blue, and yellow. It was too stylised to be any particular breed, but the snout was long, the ears droopy, the tail curled around one small back leg. It was lying on its belly with its front paws before it, like the Sphinx. This statue had turned its head slightly to one side – very un-sphinx-like. The head was less adorned than the rest of the colourful body, with only a curling green fish-hook symbol on top, and a few lines of blue beneath its eyes. There were some faint impressions of the nose and mouth. The eyes themselves were closed.

Archibald laid a finger on that long snout and stroked it gently, feeling the cool surface on his skin. It was the eyes that made it so alive, he decided, because it gave the impression of sleep. The dog almost breathed.

Sighing, Archibald made his way to the exit. He liked the dog now, he told himself, but once he took it home it would only taunt him, like the type-writer. He was almost to the store's entrance when he turned back towards the shelf that housed the dog statue. Screw it, he thought.

Rarely have the vicissitudes of one man's will resulted in the back and forth that followed. A full three times did Archibald place the dog statue back on its shelf and head towards the doors. Finally, exasperated with himself, he bought the dog and walked back home clutching it in a little paper bag.

The statue was still pretty by the time he got home. Sitting on his bed, he took it out of the bag and held it in his hands. There was something precious about the paws, and the nose. The eyes, too. Especially the eyes. Archibald put it on his desk, next to the typewriter, and stroked its little snout with a finger.

* * *

At dinner that night, the subject of the typewriter came up again.

'It's not good to leave it sitting there unused for so long,' Archibald's father said.

'It's getting used,' Archibald said as he pushed his broccoli around the plate. 'I wrote to Beatrice this afternoon.'

'Really?' Linda cut her lamb chop into precise little pieces while she digested this news.

'Was Beatrice the New Zealander?' his father asked. 'Or was that Rebecca?'

'Rebecca,' Linda said with an authoritative nod. 'Beatrice lives in Mornington, doesn't she, Rick?'

'She does.'

Archibald's father nodded over his chops. 'Ah yeah... thought it was Daylesford.'

'No, Dad.'

Archibald forked some broccoli into his mouth. The evening light patterned warm lines against the floor as it passed through the shutters.

'So...' his father began. 'Beatrice...'

'Did you post the letter, darling?' his mother interjected.

'I'll do it – y'know, I'll just do it now,' Archibald said. 'Mind if I excuse myself?'

His mother smiled and squeezed his hand. 'Go ahead, darling.'

'Not before you clear your plate,' his father said. 'That means the cutlery, too.'

Archibald Truck washed all the dishes, and the forks and knives, too.

* * *

It was mid-summer, and so it had still been sunny at six o'clock, when the Trucks had started their evening meal. It was past seven by the time Archibald left to post his letter, and the clear sky had grown crowded with clouds that brought a breeze and a cool change with them. It was a little darker than it might have been on a clear day, and the air had the quality of stained-blue glass.

At the post-box, Archibald found it difficult to release the letter. He felt its grainy texture with his thumb. It wasn't an especially important letter. Run of the mill. But he hadn't spoken to Beatrice for a while. The stresses of work had crowded her out, and he felt more confident reconnecting with ink and paper than over the phone. He breathed in the eucalyptus and focused on the whispering of leaves. The envelope slid down the side of the post-box with a muffled rustling. It was like a silent language, almost not there at all.

Almost like a whispered name.

Archibald took a long, dawdling way home, listening to the whispers of the trees. Thinking of nothing much in particular, he wondered what they were saying. He breathed the words back to the trees, in his closest approximation of their tongueless speech. Dusk was only just over the horizon as he stepped over the threshold of his parents' house.

In his room, he got out a pen and pad of paper and jotted down a few of the nonsense words he had learnt from the trees. One stood out to him particularly.

'Darandra.'

It just had a ring. More than anything else on the page, it sounded like how the breeze made him feel, like a kiss from a spirit of the air. It was a name, certainly a name, and a name belongs to a person or a place. Hunched over his desk, he *thought*. Archibald Truck thought, and his fingers itched so hard to write down his ideas that he could hardly think anymore. And so he decided that it *was* the name of a person, and that she lived on an island, that she had heard the whispers at night as she stood in the shallow waters of a lagoon, while little waves lapped around her calves, and the soft sea breeze caressed her face.

After seven pages of notes, he set up the typewriter and cleared away everything else from his desk. Except the dog. He stroked its snout with his thumb.

And at the top of the page, Archibald Truck typed in capital letters:

DARANDRA OF THE ISLAND

Perhaps you've heard of her.

* * *

He took another few weeks to complete it, writing on and off every few days, although it was only a little story. But the next story was a completely different one, and he worked on it every day, always touching the dog's nose before he started. Even when he was back teaching at the school, he wrote as much as he could. Sometimes, that was hardly anything at all. And the stress that dogged him, the long hours and disrespect, often ground his typewriter to a halt more effectively than any jammed keys ever could. And yet he continued.

He showed his stories to Beatrice, who took to attacking them with her red pen. At the end of the school year, he tried his hand at reworking that first story into a novel.

And all the while the dog kept her eyes closed, peacefully asleep.

17

The Vigil

Rachel Martin

It's my second night in the room with my mother.

She is a vision of beauty. Her face smoothed of wrinkles along with all signs of pain. Like a queen, she is laid out on sheepskin in the boat of her wooden casket. Her head gently raised on a pillow. A children's rose on her chest; her hands clasped lightly below.

I approach her body. Touch her cold pale hands. Admire the tapering of her form beneath the white sheet to the small crest of her toes.

Beside her in this chilly room the tall candles flicker in the dark so it appears to me that she breathes. Her lips slightly parted. She breathes.

I search her face in the candlelight, then tell her what I am about to do. About the letters. How I tried to read them to her while she lived but how she was too ill. There were too many. How I waited until now, when she would be able to understand.

I turn to gather the pile from the bookshelf. The final words of love. The final goodbyes.

Holding up the first sheet of paper, I draw a candle near to bring the words to life and tell her who it is from. And as I begin to read, I feel her listening.

After an hour I pause and sit a while, savouring this last night before we close the coffin lid. It's been forty-four hours since my daughter called me at three am on Russian Orthodox Easter Friday; forty-four hours since the death we had begun to doubt was coming, arrived.

'She's passed?' I'd asked into the silence.

'Yes,' the whisper came back.

Ten minutes later I'd parked in the leafy street of the house she'd lived in for forty years and joined my daughter and sister in the bedroom. The transformation was dramatic. It was true, our mother was finally at peace.

I take another letter from the pile and hold it up to the light. 'Dearest,' it begins, 'this is a letter we never want to write...' and I pause to control my tears before I continue.

It's cold in this place she has chosen to rest and I am thirsty. I consider stepping outside under the waning moon to sip from my water bottle, then I remember her last week of thirst and all mine disappears. Death came so fast and yet so slowly. I think of the last day she could swallow, a week ago, when my daughter slipped grape after grape into her mouth in the hope she would stay with us. Five grapes and after that even water was too much. We wet her tongue with cotton swabs. Moistened her lips each time we turned her body. Each time we washed and changed her. Each time she looked at us with those parched eyes, and again and again in those last four days after her gaze turned inwards and she could no longer ask.

* * *

Three-thirty a.m. The morning of her departure. The palliative care nurse arrives, enters the bedroom quietly. She performs tests and ticks boxes on a white sheet of paper:

> *Absence of respiratory movement and breath sounds for two minutes.*
> *Absence of carotid pulse for two minutes.*
> *Absence of heart sounds for two minutes.*
> *Fixed non-reactive pupils.*

The nurse already knows our plans for the body; she gathers the morphine syringes she drew up earlier and quietly leaves.

My remaining siblings arrive.

Then our death doula.

Four a.m. We turn off the heater and set up the massage table at the foot of her bed, wrap our mother in her sheet and lift her gently across.

So it begins.

With tenderness and attention to detail the death doula cleans out our mother's mouth and brushes her teeth. We wash her hair using shampoo and jugs of warm water, rinsing 'til the water runs clear, gentle streams of it, flowing from her hair into the basin below. We dry her hair carefully with the hairdryer. Pluck hair from her chin. Clean the sleep from her eyes.

Outside, the suburbs slumber under a dark starry sky but in this room of roses and oil paintings we work in silent unison. We pull back the sheet and begin the process of cleaning our mother's body, cutting away her night-gown and undergarments as we progress from face to toes. Every inch of her olive skin we rub with lavender and rosemary bath milk, removing any scent. Inside her hairless armpits. Along the length of her back and sides. Her chest and thighs. Her fine and delicate arms and wrists. Beneath her perfectly oval fingernails. Her bone-sharp hips. Her still warm abdomen. Her long legs. Her cold toes.

By the time we begin to oil this woman who raised us, rigor mortis is setting in. Now, as we turn her from back to side and back again, her torso and hips maintain their position. Slowly, careful to cover each part, my sister and I rub oil of frankincense and myrrh into her skin to purify her and to help her bridge the two worlds. Our doula anoints first our mother's face and then her heart and hands with an ointment made of gold, lavender and rose.

At last we are ready to dress her in a clean white nightgown, slide her onto a fresh sheet and lift her carefully onto the sheepskin of her artisan casket.

The dawn has come and gone in the dewy garden of our childhood home. There are six handles to the coffin and six of us to carry her. We move slowly. A sombre passage to my elder brother's van. We slide the lidless coffin inside and stand in a semi-circle before her in the overgrown wilderness. Again we recite the Lord's Prayer, as we have so often in the last weeks of her life, and this time her voice does not join ours.

It's time. I gather flowers and squeeze into the van next to the coffin to hold it steady. My back is to the cab, my legs stretched out alongside hers and a moment later my brother slides the van doors closed and we set off, stopping to buy take-away coffees from her favourite cafe on the way.

* * *

It is one a.m. In five hours my shift will end and the day will begin with a slow stream of visitors: This passage of her friends who have flowed through since noon yesterday, will flow on again tomorrow and through the funeral and on through the night to the cremation on Monday morning. Those who take part in the vigil bring spiritual readings to comfort and guide her. They sit quietly in meditation. They read aloud. They bring candles and guitars;

they come alone and in groups and they replace one another each hour until eleven p.m. when I return for the night shift, again.

On that first night, as I rolled out my sleeping bag on the couch and lay watching the candle-light dance on her face, I was reminded of how in the past people used to come and sit with the dead to receive blessings. The sanctity of it. Tonight I feel it again. Her presence in the room, the feel of angels' wings around me as they stand guard.

I move to the far side of my mother's body, step over the power cord of the cold plate that lies beneath her coffin and riffle through the pile of letters remaining. Less than a dozen to go. I feel the weight of the night, the presence of my sister at our mother's house putting the finishing touches on the coffin lid that she has painted with a life-sized angel: Wings spread protectively around the curved lid; halo made of real gold; Frida Kahlo inspired skeleton mirroring the expanse of bones our mother has become.

How long it has been since yesterday morning. A whole lifetime lived in these long, short hours in this room which has been set aside for the vigil of death. I lift a small candle to the page in front of me and I read on and on until it is done.

The candles burn and flicker. It is one twenty-seven a.m. I want to stay awake all night and look upon her queenly face while I still have the chance. Her aquiline nose. Her defined cheekbones. Her lips parted further now that rigor mortis has passed and death has relaxed her jaw. Today our death doula placed a rolled-up hand towel beneath our mother's chin to keep her mouth from opening too widely and I am grateful. Grateful her mouth is not sewn shut as is the common parlour practice.

The candles flicker and smoke twirls into the darkness. For a long time I keep watch as I imagine her reviewing her life. I will miss you my mother. The candles flicker and it is cold in this room and I slip into my sleeping bag and sleep until dawn when a gentle knocking wakes me and my shift comes to an end.

Today the funeral. And tomorrow her body will be consumed by flames.

18

The Girl Who Slept on the Edge of the Bed

Angela Jones

She ate strawberries for breakfast;
Kerouac for lunch
  Mer–lot and peanuts

She fed ravens stale bread;
the bleak beaks held it
  Feath–ered black, Elvis?

She sipped coffee by the train line;
mugged hot and black
  Ne–ver long mac

She patted dogs on the footpath:
fur coats and fleas
  Stil–ton blue cheese

She washed hands in the fountain:
lukewarm from pipes
  Con–verse tied tight

She ate dinner at night-fall:
honey chicken and lime
  Chop–sticks waste time

She read Ginsberg on the sofa
and ate naked sandwiches
   Addict-ed linguist

She slept on the edge of the bed;
duck-filled feather quilt
   Mid-dle class guilt

19

Rose among the Thorns

Merav Fima

My grandmother has been enamoured with the Song of Songs for as long as I can remember. Already as a young child, I myself became entangled in its mysterious enchantment.

I remember those eerie nights when my siblings and I slept at my grandparents' house in Ein Kerem, a serene village on the slopes of Jerusalem's hills, the stone houses enlaced with lofty pine trees. My grandmother would put us to bed in the upstairs bedroom with the vaulted ceiling and painted floor tiles singing:

> *I am asleep but my heart is awake, the voice of my beloved knocks.*
> *'Open up, my sister, my beloved, my dove, my innocent one;*
> *for dew suffuses my head, drops of the night fill my locks.'*

On those nights I would have the strangest dreams. My eyelids would grow heavy as I counted the scintillating stars, brighter than anything I ever saw in the city, and smelled the fragrance of the almond blossoms penetrating the chamber through the open window. At that moment a procession of strangers would appear to me, claiming to be my ancestors. Though they all bore some resemblance to my grandmother, I did not recognise them.

One woman had my grandmother's dimpled cheek and deep set brown eyes and wore a gold crown on her head. Another was young and freckled and sat at a small Damascene table hunched over a sewing machine, her feet rhythmically tapping the manual pedal – as though it were a piano – as her hands gracefully slid the voluminous velvet across the wooden table inlaid with mother-of-pearl. Yet another, wearing a satin gown, sat in a rose

84

garden strumming the lute. The water flowing from the fountain behind her punctuated my grandmother's humming as she rocked in her chair, waiting for us to fall asleep.

Like the women in my dreams, my grandmother wore a gold chain around her neck, with a pomegranate-shaped pendant suspended from it. Its scarlet jewels – made of garnets, my birthstone – emitted an unusual radiance. Curled up in my grandmother's lap, I couldn't resist handling it, my fingers drawn, like metal to magnet, to its cool, smooth surface. Turning the pendant over in the palm of my hand, I would ask, 'What does it say here?' She would recite the engraved verses:

> *My beloved is a locked garden, a sealed fountain;*
> *A pomegranate orchard with exquisite fruits.*

The necklace never left my grandmother's neck. She never let me try it on, no matter how much I implored. 'This necklace has been in the family for over five hundred years; one day it will be yours,' she promised, tracing the contours of my face with her soft fingers.

My grandmother, Paloma, refused to serve dinner on Friday nights, when the entire family gathered at her home to celebrate the Sabbath, until my grandfather, Solomon, finished chanting all eight chapters of the Song of Songs to her. Enthroned in his chair at the head of the table, like his name-sake, his melodious voice serenaded her at the end of every week:

> *You are beautiful, my love;*
> *You are beautiful;*
> *Your eyes are doves.*

The flickering flames atop the tall silver candlesticks accentuated Savta Paloma's high cheekbones and noble neck. Caressing her hand, Sabba Solomon would gaze into her brown eyes with a tenderness that always moved me to tears.

Exasperated by the length of the ceremony, my mother would interrupt my grandfather's recitation:

'The children are getting hungry!'

'They can wait. They are no longer babies,' was my grandmother's usual response. Winking at my grandfather, she'd continue, 'Let them be nourished by their grandparents' love, a love upon which the world's very existence depends.' I always found my grandparents' connection inspiring and hoped that one day I, too, would love and be loved.

Setting the leather-bound tome on the white tablecloth embroidered with silver thread, my grandfather would rise to his feet and kiss my grandmother's outstretched hand. Her dimple would become apparent as she returned his smile and reciprocated his praise. All those gathered around the table would then join in greeting the guardian angels and sanctifying the Sabbath with the blessing over the wine. I could almost see the angels, donning translucent gowns of white light, hovering around the table, their iridescent wings fluttering.

Only then would the steaming delicacies be brought to the table – lamb tagine with dried fruits, walnuts, and caramelised onions seasoned with cinnamon, cardamom, and cloves, rice with slivered almonds and raisins, and a green salad dressed with pomegranate vinaigrette, freshly extracted from the fruit of the tree in the garden. The food was as delectable to the palate as to the eye, its aromas suffusing the dining room. These were the dishes I craved whenever I visited my grandmother, foods that my mother never made at home. 'It takes far too much work and I really don't have the time to spare.'

When my grandparents approached their golden anniversary, I sought an appropriate gift to mark the occasion. I wandered into the Old City of Jerusalem through Zion Gate and walked the narrow cobblestone alleyways to the Cardo, the Roman marketplace at the heart of the Jewish Quarter, dotted with a row of classical columns surmounted by ornate capitals. The cream-coloured Jerusalem stone refracted the golden sunlight striking the statuesque buildings.

I knew that I would recognise the ideal gift when I saw it, and soon stumbled upon a small gallery – wedged between a jeweller's studio and a ceramics cooperative – with bold abstract paintings hanging on either side of the arched doorway.

Bells chimed as I entered the vaulted chamber with muffled steps. My eyes jumped from canvas to canvas, replete with vividly coloured birds in flight, until I was drawn to a lone painting on the opposite wall of the gallery that differed in its small scale and subdued tonality from all the others. Framed in silver, it depicted a majestic pomegranate tree with luscious red fruits and a pair of white doves nestled in its branches. 'This must be it.' I knew how my grandmother relished the pomegranate tree in her garden, wrapping each individual fruit blossom to protect it from insects, and how much she prized her necklace. I couldn't help but think of the pair of doves on the paper as my grandparents, eternally faithful in their love.

I had thought that the gallery was vacant, but as I examined the painting a woman of slight stature waltzed across the floor. Her long blond hair illumined her face like sunbeams and she lit up the dim space with every step she took.

'Isn't it beautiful?' she asked. 'It's one of my favourites.'

'Yes, it's magnificent,' I stammered. 'I am looking for a gift for my grandparents' fiftieth anniversary. They will love its elegant simplicity.'

'I'm sure they will,' affirmed the gallery owner.

'My grandfather's name is Solomon and my grandmother is Paloma – a dove. It's as though this painting was made specially for them.'

'I had a feeling about it when I painted it. I always like to have an idea of the person for whom the artwork is intended in mind at the outset and knew that the doves would have special significance. Do you know that the painting contains the entire Song of Songs?'

My heart skipped a beat. I hadn't noticed. I took a step forward and observed the work up close. I could now see that the jagged lines delineating the leaves, birds, and branches consisted of miniscule Hebrew script in coloured ink, meticulous work that must have taken days of concentration to complete.

I read the words constituting the round red fruits topped with coronets:

> *Let us rise and head to the vineyards to see if the vine has budded,*
> *if the vine-blossom has opened, if the pomegranates have flowered;*
> *there I will give you my love.*

I felt a shiver running down my spine. There could not be a more perfect gift.

The woman extended her hand to me. 'I am Bina Ravel, by the way. What's your name?'

I hesitated, but somehow knew that I could trust her.

'My name is Kitra Vardi.' An electrifying energy emanated from her fingertips as we shook hands.

'Kitra Vardi is a wonderful name for a poet,' she exclaimed. 'Why don't you come back here tomorrow evening? I will be hosting a gathering of artists and writers and would like to introduce you to them. I will have the painting all wrapped up and ready for you to take home to your grandparents then.'

With that, she pirouetted across the room to the next customer, her sequined bell sleeves swirling around her torso like outspread wings. I did not know how she had intuited my most profound desire to become a poet, but it was then that I started taking my ambition seriously and cherishing the uniqueness of my name Kitra, a name that had until then been the source of tremendous grief and countless taunts by classmates mocking its Aramaic origin. I soon became a regular visitor to Bina's gallery, bringing her scattered verses and polished poems to read.

My grandmother's hands shook as she unwrapped the parcel. 'It's a very thoughtful gift,' she said. 'Of all my grandchildren, you have always had the most kindred spirit.'

The painting hung on a prominent wall in my grandparents' living room and I admired it every time I came for a visit. When I turned twenty-five and was still not married, my twin sisters, Tiferet and Ateret, convinced me that I needed to take urgent action as I might be running out of time. My grandmother reassured me that my intended was on his way. 'You've got such exotic beauty, Kitra, I have no doubt that you will soon meet a deserving young man.' She urged me to try the method she had used to conjure my grandfather more than half a century before. 'Read the Song of Songs in its entirety for the next forty days. It is a sacred tradition in our family. Just don't tell your mother that I told you to do this. She'll say that I am brainwashing you with my primitive superstitions, even though she herself used this very same method to meet your father.'

Though I considered it highly improbable that my mother would have engaged in such practices in her youth and was unsure if I believed in the power of the incantation, I thought that it wouldn't hurt to try. 'Don't worry about it, Savta. It will be our secret.' I sealed the pact with a kiss on her lined cheek.

I spent the next forty nights reading the Song of Songs from beginning to end before turning off the lights in my bedroom. Perched on my narrow bed, I savoured the sound of every syllable I enunciated. I tried to imagine what my beloved would look like and how we would sit around the dinner table on Friday nights reciting these very same verses to each other.

I am the lily of Sharon, the rose of the valleys.
Like a rose among the thorns, so is my beloved among the maidens.

Perhaps I was the rose among the thorns, unable to truly open my heart to another; perhaps I had put up a prickly façade, internalising the rose's properties bequeathed by my surname Vardi.

I always waited until my parents had gone to bed before beginning the recitation, tired of hearing my mother telling me that it would be wise to complete my education before seeking a spouse. But instead of conjuring my beloved, the procession of ancestors reappeared in my dreams. I usually forgot about them by the time I woke up in the morning, but would continue feeling unsettled all day long.

When nearly a year had passed and I wasn't yet engaged, I decided to take more drastic measures. Reading the Song of Songs had proved to be insufficient; it would behove me to transcribe the text in order to contemplate every letter. I made my way to the Old City, where my feet instinctively led me to Bina's gallery, and asked her to teach me how to create my own micrography, like the one she had sold me several years before as a gift for my grandparents.

'The technique is really quite simple; you just have to be in the right state of mind.'

'What do you mean?'

'Start by envisioning an image from the Song of Songs.'

'How about *the rose among the thorns*?'

'That will do. Begin by outlining the rose in pencil and decide where you would like the biblical text to begin and end. Use coloured pens to inscribe the verses along the outline. Once the ink is dry you can erase the pencil marks, et voilà!'

I made several sketches, my handwriting becoming more compact with each attempt, but felt that it was all mere craft and artifice. Bina examined my drawings. 'They lack soul. I want you to do this on the next full moon. Meditate on the following verses from the Zohar, *The Book of Radiance*, and its mystical interpretation of the Song of Songs:

A song that is holy of holies
As the highest divine name is crowned by it
Because all of its words are love and joy

'I thought you weren't supposed to study the Zohar before the age of forty. Isn't it dangerous?'

'Not if it is done with the proper intention,' Bina reassured me. 'Besides, the best things in life come at a risk.' I was willing to risk it for the prospect of marriage.

Sitting at my desk, I closed my eyes and contemplated the verses Bina had dictated. The brilliance of the full moon penetrated my eyelids. Each ray of moonlight dissolved into the seven colours of the spectrum as it traversed the prism of my retina.

I opened my eyes and the white page glowed in the luminescence of the moonlight, forming a halo around the rose petals I had unknowingly traced with my eyes closed. I felt my own words flowing out of my heart, comingling with the sacred Scriptures, as the ink flowed from the pen. I had never before shown my poetry to anyone but Bina. She was the first person who ever believed in me, the only one who encouraged me to pursue my passion.

Still now, I sought to conceal my poetic words in miniscule script illegible to the naked eye, ashamed of the desperation and vulnerability they articulated.

> *Thou shall not take God's name in vain*
> *Why did you betray me?*
> *Why did you breathe the four letters of the holiest name*
> *LOVE אהבה*
> *Crowning the common name?*
>
> *You did not allow the Shekhinah to dwell among us*
> *And your soul did not cling to mine with the kiss of your mouth*
> *For you are a wall, a locked garden*
>
> *You have sought only to nestle your head*
> *In my fragrant chest*
> *To caress my dark skin*
>
> *But my heart is awake and your heart is deaf to the throbbing between*
> *my breasts.*

This was my first poem to take concrete form, the words shaping the rose's red petals, green leaves, and brown thorns. As I placed the Hebrew letters side by side on the paper, I felt a burning sensation in my fingertips and an unknown warmth in my heart.[1]

---

1   This story was a finalist in the *Tiferet* literary journal's 2019 Fiction Contest.

20

Skin Deep

Miguela Considine

It's the first day of school.

Bettina sees them as she stands before the mirror, smelling of Johnson & Johnson, her long wet hair waiting to be combed until it's sleek and touching her bottom. She hates the brushing the most. Her hair always ends up a tangled mess, the teeth of the comb yanking at her scalp so painfully. She wants nothing more than to have a cute short haircut like Madeline.

'Girls are meant to have long hair, Tia,' Dad says. Tia sulks. She pouts. She wants to suck on her thumb, but she's not a baby anymore, so she bites at her fingernails instead.

Her nails dig at her elbows absently as she waits for the brushing. Then she sees them in the mirror: the little red dots scattered across her chest, her arms, her legs, her face. They weren't there before; they're not like the big red marks on her elbows and knees from scratching too much. And now that she's noticed them, it feels like her whole body has little people underneath the surface, like they're marching underneath in two by two and pushing up against her skin, making those little red dots erupt.

'Mum!' She screams, running out to the kitchen in nothing but her undies.

'*Hay naku!* Tia, get back in your room, you have chickenpox. Go, go, *Susmaria!*' Mum shoos her away, away from the baby, back into her room, where she sits on the bed and stares at the little invading dots in horror.

The next two weeks she is stuck at home, missing out on the much-anticipated princess day at school. After every bath, Mum slathers horrible-smelling purple stuff all over her and she has to stand in the bathroom, turning in circles for ten minutes with her arms out until it's all dry. And it itches so bad, the little people under her skin. They keep her up at night with their marching and their pushing and their prickling; she swears they're doing it on purpose, so Mum and Dad make her wear socks on her hands all the time to stop her from scratching but she takes the socks off to scratch anyway, and when she closes the bedroom door she chooses one red dot on her chest, where Mum and Dad can't see, and she picks away at it, so sure that if she can just flip it over and see the back of it she'll catch one of the little people in the act and she can ask them to stop what they're doing. But she can never quite get under it; it just gets bigger and uglier and scabbier and bloodier until it's a big ugly scar that never goes away – then, the red dots are gone, except now her baby sister has it, but that's fine, she's a baby, she's meant to get it. The itching stops and the red dots are gone and the little people under her skin are gone and that's all that matters.

(Had to count for something, right? Because the girls at school – they thought her long hair was stupid and called her funny names and insisted her mum was Chinese, not Filipino, and that she couldn't play with them. The boys, they took her in, they liked that she knew who Sonic and X-Men were, and they didn't mind that sometimes she wanted to be Princess Leia and sometimes she wanted to be Luke Skywalker. It didn't last – she had to move schools and start all over again. The girls were nicer there and some of the boys pulled her braid and they started to call her Hairy Maclary, like the dog. She didn't understand at first, except that her last name was McClary. She thought it was because of her braid.)

'No, dummy.' Katie points at Tia's legs one lunchtime. 'It's because of your legs!'

She glances down at her legs – these little toothpick-like things stretched out on the grass, a few bruises from where she's constantly bumping into things, a scab on one knee from a fall the week before. Now that Tia looks at them – actually *looks* at them – she can see the dark hair that covers them. It's darker than the hair on her arms and as she quickly glances at the paler legs of her friends on either side, it's darker and thicker than their hair, too.

She quickly pulls her knees up to her chest, trying to drag her dress over her legs to cover them. Her thumb's in her mouth, but she's not sucking it; she's not a baby, she's just chewing on the nail, worrying away at the jagged skin.

It's the little people again. They must have done it. They must have pushed the hairs out. Surely she would have felt it? Why hadn't she felt it?

That night, Tia asks Mum to help her get rid of the hair. Mum – with her beautifully soft, smooth, always moisturised darker skin that smells like coconut – gently takes her hand and guides her to the bathroom, where she runs a bath and shows her the razor.

'Always use hot water and soap.'

Mum shows Tia how to lather the soap along her legs and slowly bring the razor up along her long shin bone. She winces when the razor cuts into her flesh, the blood gushing up and mixing with the soap until it's frothy and pink.

'Beauty is pain, Tia,' Mum tuts, as she holds a flannel to the cut. 'No pain, no gain.'

It's the sign Dad keeps with all his cycling trophies. No pain, no gain. No guts, no glory.

After her bath, Tia marvels at her new shiny legs. She uses some of Mum's moisturiser – to make sure she doesn't get a rash, Mum's orders – and she can't stop running her hands up and down the smooth planes.

They stop calling her Hairy McClary.

Shaving becomes a routine, every four days. The little people seem to make the hair come back faster, though, and she starts having to shave every two days, then every day, but she's determined to make sure her legs stay silky and smooth and hair-free.

The little red dots come back, too.

They're unnoticeable at first, hidden behind her fringe. It's only when she's in front of the mirror, pushing the hair back to brush them out that she sees them, that splattering of red across her forehead.

'Just sweat pimples.' Dad nods with surety, sweeping her fringe back into place. 'Make sure you wear your fringe back when you're at soccer, they'll go away.'

But they don't go away. The little people work hard to make sure the red dots stay, growing, multiplying. Then, the day before her uncle's wedding – where she and her little sister are meant to be flower girls – she wakes up with a massive ugly red thing on the side of her nose.

Dad drags her in front of the mirror in the bathroom and they stare at that red thing together. It's huge, the size of a ten-cent piece. She can feel it throbbing and aching. There's something small and white at the centre of it, ready to explode.

'Okay, never, ever pop a pimple,' Dad is saying, holding a flannel under the hot water tap. 'I knew a kid in school, he always had pimples. He popped one just before school, and you know what happened? He died, right there in class, because the pus travelled to his brain and killed him.'

Tia is staring at the flannel, at Dad's hands, at the big red thing next to her nose. That thing, this thing the little people put there, could kill her?

'You grab a flannel, get it as hot as you can handle, and just take the top off the pimple, like this.' And he's put the flannel on the big red thing, and she's closing her eyes and biting her tongue trying not to shout out because she's no baby, beauty is pain, but the flannel is so hot, and he's holding it there and holding it and pressing it and holding it and finally he lets go and her whole cheek is red but the red dot just looks angrier, the white pus bigger, and Dad mutters under his breath and tries the flannel again.

When the flannel doesn't work, he switches to tea tree oil, but that doesn't work either. The giant pimple refuses to budge. Tia stares at her face in the mirror, can see tears in her own eyes, but she doesn't make a sound, won't let those tears fall.

Finally, Dad pinches his forefinger and his thumb around the stubborn pimple.

'Don't you ever do this, okay?'

And then he squeezes.

In all the wedding photos, Tia's face is miserable. They'd tried to cover the big brown scab on the side of her nose with Mum's foundation, but it was too dark, too cakey. It just makes the scab stand out even more.

(It was the opening of the floodgates. The little people were working overtime, ensuring that there were new red explosions across her face constantly – some with big pus-filled centres, others deep under the skin, painful, like they'd set little rock-filled fires along her chin. She didn't have it so bad, like other girls in her year whose entire faces were red and purple from the acne, but it was persistent, and she couldn't stop herself from picking at it, from poking at them, from using a pin to pierce them, from standing in front of the mirror and trying to force her little tormentors from her skin until it was pockmarked and scarred and scabbed, and if Dad asked if she was picking at them she denied it, she just said she was scratching,

she was itchy, because it was true. She tried to cover it up a few times at school, sneaking some of Mum's compact foundation, but their skin tones were too differ-ent and she didn't know she was meant to blend it at the neckline and it ended up looking worse.)

'Side effects include blood in the stool, dry skin, itching –', the doctor reads from the sheet of paper as Tia chews at her nail. She doesn't care about the side effects. She just wants it gone. '– and possible depression and suicidal ideation.'

'Sorry, what was that last part?' Dad leans forward in his chair, frowning. Tia's teeth pause, her thoughts racing, *shut up Dad shut up Dad don't ruin this for me –*

'Oh, it's very uncommon, just something I have to warn patients about.' The doctor turns the page to show Dad, then shifts his eyes to Tia. 'Have you ever experienced anything like that? Depression, thoughts of self-harm?'

She pulls her sleeves over her hands, sitting on them to stop chewing on her fingernails, to stop the tremor in her right hand, a tremor that would stay with her for the rest of her life. She doesn't want to tell them how her right hand started twitching non-stop three weeks before, after she found out the guy she liked didn't like her back; how she filled a page of her sketch-book with etched scrawls, begging for help, asking what was wrong with her, if she'd ever find someone, why she was so ugly; how sometimes in the shower she'd take a pair of scissors to draw meticulous little lines on her inner biceps, on her thighs, on her hips, anywhere easy to hide but easy to see when she looked in the mirror.

Beneath it all, she could still feel them, scratching back at her.
'No,' she says, finally.

(The Roaccutane worked, for a time – her skin was the clearest it'd been in years. On her face, that was. Her arms and legs were dry, with large scabs from her con-stant, incessant scratching. She shat blood. And she was cutting herself more, sitting on the cold bathroom tiles to draw messier lines, deeper lines. But they couldn't tell. No one could. She would put on her biggest, goofiest smile and make them laugh. Because she wasn't a kid anymore and while she pretended like she was aloof, that she was the cool kid who didn't care, she –)

'You're different from the other girls, y'know.'

It's three weeks into uni, in a different town, over a thousand kilometres away from her friends, her childhood, her life. She can be a different person here, she decides in her car – one of the *cool* girls, one of the *hot* girls who goes to parties and drinks and has a boyfriend.

It's nice to have dreams.

He has blue eyes.

'They're all the same, they're pretty or they're cute, but you? You're sexy.'

Tia likes the way he says it. *Sexy*. No one has ever called her sexy before. She tries the word on, standing in front of the mirror in the bathroom, turning her body to different angles to get new shapes – her hips this way, her tits pointing another. She finds one perfect shape: arched back, making a little gap appear between her thighs, but pouts when a ripple of fat is pushed up by the traitors under her skin, right by her shoulder blade. She has to stretch to make it disappear until she is perfectly flat.

It's raining when he fucks her the first time.

'You should cut your hair,' he says, playing with her braid. 'Can I take you to a hairdresser?'

Dad's face is flat when he sees her hair. It's sleek and shiny and cut just above her shoulders. It's the healthiest it's ever looked.

'...what do you think?'

Dad just sighs. 'It looks nice.'

Within six months, Tia moves in with the blue-eyed boy. Dad doesn't approve of him, but Tia doesn't care – he makes her skin, her heart, sing. She's never felt anything like it before.

'You should do bikini competitions,' he says one day, pointing at a poster at the pub. The woman on the poster is toned, tanned, blonde.

'What? No. I can't do that.'

'Yeah, you look great in a bikini. Trust me.'

She's doubtful at first. She starts a diet. She starts to run again. She practices walking in heels.

She qualifies for the finals.

'See? I told you!'

She cuts down to eating just an apple, a salad, a can of tuna. She runs and goes to the gym for an hour, every day. She buys a self-tanning kit and stands in the bathroom, waiting for it to air dry before she can put her clothes back on. She learns how to do stage makeup in under twenty minutes.

She comes second.

She sees him hitting on other contestants.

'You should do more of these!' He tells her.

She enters every competition she can.

Tia drops down to a size six. She always places in the top five but never wins. He tags along to all the competitions as her manager – even to the finalist-only photoshoots at faraway locations.

Underneath her skin, it burns ice-hot to her bones as she slathers the fake tan over and over and over and over –

(Her first suicide attempt was after she found out he cheated on her. Forty ibu-profen tablets meant a quick overnight stay in emergency where they just mon-itored her, gave her some stuff for nausea, and said she probably had borderline personality disorder. Didn't answer anything about the burning under her skin, the nothingness she felt deep within. It took her two years to finally find the courage to leave him, because she didn't think she'd ever find someone to call her beautiful until an English backpacker crossed her path and told her that there were seven billion people in the world, so why was she letting one childish boy hold her back? She packed her bags the next day and moved back in with Mum and Dad, then back to Sydney three months later. She could be anyone again, anyone she wanted to be. Betty the professional. Tina the sassy promo model. Tia the nerdy gym girl. Whoever she wanted.)

'You're looking so good!' They say.

'What's your secret?!' They ask.

Tia smiles and Tia laughs and Tia accepts the compliments, but she knows as she stands in the bathroom that the only truth she'll find is in the mirror before her. Mirrors don't lie; they only reflect what you need to see.

And all she sees is blemished skin and a body that isn't perfect.

'But you've lost so much weight!' They cry. 'How did you do it?'

Hunched over a computer screen, too anxious about work to eat; skipping breakfast, skipping lunch, hardly eating dinner, calories coming only from alcohol to drown out the desire to tear off her skin with her bare hands; losing over twelve kilos in four months.

'Your skin is glowing!'

Lined up like little soldiers on the vanity, bottles of products with chemical names: niacinamide, salicylic acid, hyaluronic acid, azelaic acid, lactic acid, Vitamin C, rosehip oil, retinoids. Tia counts off the names like a mantra as she doles out the drops, one by one, to put them on her screaming, burning skin.

The day has gone like every other: the failed attempt at deep breathing, as prescribed by the psych. A thirty-minute run around the park. Another panic attack, trapped in the shower. Her skincare regime to help settle and soothe her aching skin.

As she stands before the vanity, putting her armour on to brave the day, she lets out a breath.

Primer. Foundation. Concealer. Bronzer and highlighter and eyebrow powder, a brush of mascara and eyeliner and translucent powder to set. All with a light touch to achieve that no-makeup makeup look.

Beauty is pain.

But she knows pain.

She puts on the final piece: a lipstick of deep red.

The little people are clamouring, whispering, scratching, biting, but she hushes them.

Tia could handle another day.

21

Put Simply

Les Wicks

Got up from my prayers,
had half a hash cookie
& an *Old Lions* gin swindle.

Played some music
then watched *Natural Born Killers*
from end to beginning.

It was so cold outside
the possum shared a laksa with me
then loaned me his coat.

The world has fallen.
I should have stayed quiet…
admissions like these only hasten decomposition.

22

Solitude

Sarah Arber

Rolling over, switching off the alarm; it seems such an effort these days. I am grateful for the sweet sound as it kicks me from my dreams. *What were they again?...* It is better than the jarring, unceremonious awakening brought on by a five-year-old.

Groaning out of bed and into the shower, the questions start.

Knock, knock. 'Mum, can I watch the TV?'

'Are you dressed Lyra...?' Silence, she is gone. I guess that's a no.

Steam from the shower caresses my face as I slip in, dancing away from its heat; until eventually, like a frog set to boil, I can withstand it. I try to wash away the weight of it all.

Not a glimpse of an adult in weeks. Nor an utterance of conversation.

'Mum, can you sign my diary, please?' Riane's voice drifts through the bedroom door.

'I'm not dressed mate.'

Night lingers in the dawn. My feet slide along the tiles. Not functional yet. I am wary; a gloomy unease has settled in the recesses of this place. Sombre spectres, shadows of my past, figures of my torment; my derelictions.

Coffee to ease the pain. All my world for a coffee.

There is no silence here; it wounds me, the din of childish yammering. Each of them scrambling about me, grotty, clamouring, reaching, a tangle of viscous saliva and snot. The house is full, it overflows with their vindictive presence.

Their racket breathes life into the ghostly occupants of this place. They toy with each child's note; they sit with it, inhale it, and bide their time with it. Annihilating humanity, turning fourth the husk-like formations which remain. They become beings of beauteous deformity, noise and reproach.

I make their sandwiches, then my coffee. Pants on, hair up, socks, shoes. *Keys, where are they?* In the car. One, two, three, four. None forgotten.

Off they go, into the sanctuary of the school gates... I am home, home again. The silence is deafening. The shadows fill the void, encroaching on me. I shrivel before them.

This is all you're good for now. Nothing else.

Beginning almost imperceptibly, there is a familiar note, a ringing in my ears. Chiming creeps in. Amplified in the silence. Grabbing at my psyche. An intimate friend, bringing a queer kind of comfort. Its resonance weighs on me, a blight on my mind; and I begin.

Start at the front: move room to room, scrape up the leavings from the floor. Shift left, shift right, remove all that is out of place. Work your way to the back.

Reminiscent of the desolation behind me, I long for what lies ahead. The ringing intensifies.

The hazards of a messy childhood home are lessened with a clean floor.

Menial tasks providing vacancy of perception, a welcome distraction from the incessant pealing note. It creates a rift in this place of childish delight and parental fulfillment. A corruption of my reality; a concoction of truth fabricated for them.

Start at the front: vacuum in hand, ravaging the excreta left in their wake. Swipe it this way, swipe it that way; neat rows of clean carpet pile up, one after another. Work your way to the back.

Finally, breaking a sweat, a worn body and a stagnant mind.

It's all you're good for, there is no view to your humanity.

The rooms grow dull; pristine, yet dull. I move them ever closer to their true form: farcical perfection; a brilliant façade, propping up the lives of the monstrosities who rule this place. It brings them love, and an unending sense of entitlement.

Start at the front: bucket, hot water, soap, mop. Swipe left, swipe right. Kitchen, bathroom, a shine on each floor; it is satisfying, a delight.

Their presence cleansed at last, drowned beneath suds and flowing water.

There is no solace in this place.

The blight upon my mind hangs, lingering in its resonance. Spectres, tendrils, reach into its depths. Toying with my sanity. I hum to the tune. The sound echoes within me, thrumming at my existence.

Start at the front: dragging filth-encrusted clothing to the laundry, in it goes, powder; beep, beep, beep... beep. Water flowing freely, fifty minutes.

Kitchen, while I wait. Plates bottom left; bowls bottom right; cups and glasses top right; plastics top left; cutlery drawer; dishwasher tablet. Beep, beep, and water flows.

Cooking, while I wait. Five veg, cut with a perfect edge. In a pot, beef for iron, olive oil, brown it for flavour, salt-reduced stock, pepper: a well-rounded meal.

This is all you're good for. This is now, what it will be forever, receiving solicitations, and giving in to their needs.

These tiny creatures passed from my womb, through blood and ichor, into the cool warmth of my arms. Ensconced in a love of mutilated defilement. At their emergence, the knell sounds for the first time, reverberating through the entirety of my life from that moment. No going back, forever marching to someone else's tune. A musical intonation for my tale of woe.

Happiness, all will be endured, for an assurance of their happiness.

BEEP. The wait is over, washing complete.

Start at its end: Reach right to the back, into the depths of the machine's gaping maw. Pull out each soggy piece, a heavy drop into the basket.

Lug its weight outside, its hanging time. String them up, one by one. The line sags, dripping, cold, wet.

A fate you have not yet met.

Reaching its crescendo for the day, the note tolls at fever pitch. One final push, to bring me to my last encore. I steady my breath, step back from the corpses of our clothing hung perfectly from the line.

Not today.

Keys in my pocket, I tiptoe to the door. Tranquillity overcomes me, its stark contrast is staggering. Breath steady, I sneak forward, gripping the doorhandle, turning it with utmost care; in fear of unsettling the spooks. The door opens, only a sliver, I slip through. Unnerved by my existence beyond these walls, I scurry to the car.

There they are. At the school gates. One, two, three, four. What a relief to see them all. Smiling faces, cleansed of the refuse imbued by the spectral depredations of our habitation.

Home again, the din of their babbling pains me, there is no escape. The house brims with their presence, and I begin.

I serve their dinner, make my cuppa. Dishes, shower, bath, teeth.
Unending servitude.

'Goodnight my sweet prince,' I whisper to Riane, pulling him close, a kiss on the cheek. A dull thrum strikes at my subconscious.

Love, ardent, true, swells from the depths of my psyche. It sits, just there, on the surface, festering, waiting. A wraithlike shadow wrenched fourth, into what little space is left... the very last piece of myself...

'Mum! You've gotta let me go.' Riane whines.

'Oh, sorry, I was daydreaming.' I smile down at him and wink. 'I could hold you here forever.'

23

Love Job

Ben Mason

On his first day back, Lewis returned to work early in the hope of catching Devon for an early morning coffee, but the chefs hadn't seen him. Outside shouts directed him to a courtyard ruckus. Hairy Harry waved a screwdriver over Janice, who shouted at him to put it down. Lewis rushed outside. Hairy hid the screwdriver behind his back. 'Lewie, it's not me fault.' His teeth were yellow, bent and rotten, like old wood palings turned to shit on a forgotten farm.

'The screwdriver, Hairy.'

'They won't give us a feed.'

'So you scare the shit outta poor, old Janice?'

Hairy's face had a permanent quiver, so it was the locked stillness that gave away his shame. In exchange for the screwdriver, Janice agreed to give Hairy a take-away. In exchange for the food, Hairy agreed to a week's self-exile. And in exchange for the peace – at Janice's insistence – Lewis did his best at sounding sincere while explaining to the homeless man how important it was, how necessary it was – he was mimicking Janice now, causing Hairy to giggle – how the whole fricken world might end, if Hairy didn't use his Health Care Card for a feed. Hairy started explaining the situation – Centrelink, address issues – but Lewis gently shushed him.

'I know, mate. It's bullshit. But it's the way it is.'

The big feller went for a hug and there was nothing to do but let it happen. Hairy's particular brand of homelessness hadn't changed: a mixture of goon, stale tobacco and infection. As he limped down the cobblestones, there was also a strong scent of urine.

* * *

Janice organised supermarket seconds while mumbling into the volunteer sheets.

'Picking up habits off the customers, Jan?'

'Clients.'

'You know what I think of that word.'

She pushed her glasses down her nose. 'Call me old again and I'll thump you.'

'Six weeks away and the place turns to shit?'

'Get your backpacking stories over with.'

He ran through the clichés of Central America: the temples in Guatemala, the friendly people in Nicaragua and diving in Honduras. He asked how the community kitchen – they weren't allowed to say soup kitchen anymore – had been.

'Good. I need you to do a couple of hundred eggs. Then you're dishwashing. By yourself.'

'By myself? Where's Dev?'

She pushed her glasses up and turned to the volunteer sheets. 'Not coming in.'

'When did he last miss a day?'

'Lewis, I need the eggs done before eleven. And the chefs have put dishes out.'

The eggs were set out in dozens on the steel table. He was deflated that Dev wouldn't be in, that he'd miss out on their kitchen banter. Dev was head dish-pig. Short and tubby with a snowflake beard and googly eyes, a Sainters cap and a not-quite-right look that barred him from market employment. Like a villain in a kid's Christmas film, Lewis had first thought.

Lewis hadn't been able to land a paid job. Before university, when he was a labourer, his aberrations were covered by hard work, a willingness to do as told and being far away from the tools, like the battler on the footy side who tackles well but can't be trusted kicking the footy. Pubs and call centres never called back. He didn't show initiative. Didn't put things back properly. Couldn't follow the script. Asked too many questions. So he applied to volunteer at The Mission.

On that first day, they paired him with Dev, who squirted and sorted plates into the dishwasher, while directing Lewis to check, dry and put away. Back of house was packed floor to ceiling: spatulas and other surgical instruments hung from hooks, drawers pulled out from everywhere and bowls and plates stacked on top of each other. Searching for the home of an especially odd instrument, Lewis circled the room like a lost ant. A straight-faced glare from a chef made him panic. And there was Dev. Leant on the dishwasher, crossed arms and snickering. The glaring chef now grinned and winked. 'You have boss who is sadistic, Lewis.'

He learnt that you could ask Dev the same question ten times, and he'd answer same as the first. Didn't get short, didn't complain to others and didn't throw his head back and stomp his foot. Nerves settled. The shifts quietened and they chatted. Dev drew pictures, wrote poetry and stories. Had an apartment in St Kilda. He ripped the piss out of Lewis when he found out he barracked for the Pies. They started going to games and catching up for coffees outside work. At first Lewis kidded himself that the meetings were an extension of the altruistic commitment of volunteer work. But over time the habits developed significance not unlike ritual, where the usual preoccupations of life floated away with his ego. He came to depend on the meetings.

'Lewis, you've put all the eggs in one bucket.' Janice's voice punched.

He noticed two other containers under the table. 'I can just pour them over.'

'Leave it. I'll do it.'

'Where's Dev, Jan?'

'The chefs are onto desserts. People have started eating.' She nodded to the kitchen.

He pretended not to be offended. He set up around the dishwasher, making the space clean and organising the dishes. There was an abstract line in the tiles he never liked the dishes to push past. When walking down the street, Lewis liked to hit every line on the pavement. Sometimes he'd be with mates and miss one. He couldn't turn back and hit it – that would be weird – but a missed line could mean he wouldn't feel right for hours.

He armed the high-pressured hose and fired at stuck-on brownie bits. It soothed him. Janice was under the pump because she'd taken over as interim manager since the last one – Karen – had quit. Ordinarily, Janice was a volunteer, a Toorak wife in five days a week. On top of that, a temp worker was covering for the head chef, who'd also quit. As if that wasn't enough, the two front-of-house staff – Nhalid and Brent – had been sacked, since it was argued that volunteers could do the job. As a result, threats, abuse and blood noses spiked. To those on the ground level, this was predictable. Nhalid and Brent had scored the jobs via job networking agencies after long stints unemployed. They loved it, interacting with customers, which was a delicate and skilled task. If the customers weren't homeless, they lived across the road in the flats. They were volatile. Generally, volunteers only came in one day a week, and so didn't have the built relationships that could de-escalate situations. Not that this was filed in any report.

Janice's hands were planted on the open counter, as she barked to the chefs over the thrum of the dishwasher. Lewis ceased the high-pressured hose and called her. She held out an upturned index finger and continued barking. More dishes came. Pushing well passed the abstract line in the tiles. A vibration took over Lewis's leg so hard he thought it might jackhammer the floor. He placed his hand on his diaphragm and slowed his breathing.

Janice's address finished and she turned to exit.

'Janice!' Diners turned their heads.

She looked at him like she couldn't believe he had the nerve, and she grunted through clenched teeth. 'Lewis – for God's sake – what?'

'Devon?'

Time was something that would crush Janice if she stood still. But there she was – frozen. Her lips zipped into a flat line. Realising she held sensitive information Lewis didn't; appreciating she would have to do something about that. 'I'll lunch with you. When it dies down.'

'Jan...'

Another heap of dishes pushed through.

'After.'

He moved trays to the dishwasher and attacked the giant soup pots crusted with pumpkin and cauliflower soup. Was it a mistake to come back? No. This was a love job, above politics. That was the promise he made to himself six months ago, when people started to leave and he considered his own position. The organisation had hired an efficiency expert. This prick had economic rationalism built into his stick-insect skeletal structure, firing out his rimless glasses. Karen's words at her goodbye drinks still rocked him: 'It's a fucking joke. Every other café on this street has an owner doing sixty-hour weeks. This parasite sits upstairs on his six-figure salary thinking up KPIs. It doesn't work.'

Was his blind servitude to the job something that *he* just did for *himself?* Something that wouldn't change anything; or worse, helped keep things the way it was? But, he'd answered, surely, these were people in need, and he was providing a service. He should stay. It was above politics.

He'd caught up with the dishes. Only a few loiterers were still eating. Lewis checked his watch and chucked the tea towel into the washing basket.

* * *

Janice got the cauliflower soup, Lewis the lasagna. Even though it rained outside, it was away from prying ears and one table was pushed against the brick wall, protected from the elements. He untied his apron and laid it over the back of his chair.

'Jesus, you look like a Jackson Pollack. What's the point in an apron?'

He clenched a sauce-striped clump of shirt. 'Sell it to ya?'

'I should call your mother.'

'There's only so much Dev can teach.'

She smiled. He waited for her to speak, but she didn't. He dropped his cutlery on the plate. 'Jan –'

'He's been admitted to a mental hospital.'

'You're fucking kidding?'

'I don't know much.'

'Did he self-admit?'

'No.'

'Fuck. What happened, why did they –'

'I don't know.'

'Well… have you even been to visit him?'

'Yes, Lewis, I have.'

'Fuck.' He bit his thumb. 'Sorry, Jan. That wasn't cool, I'm just –'

'I know.'

'I shouldn't have gone backpacking.'

'Piss off, Lewis.'

He pushed his food away. He stood up and walked in circles, hands held behind his head. Rain spat in his face. 'Something must have happened.' His voice was too loud.

'Well, actually, the week after you left,' – she swirled figure eights into her soup – 'He had an argument with one of the chefs.'

'And?'

'And nothing. It was harmless. Something to do with where plates went.'

'And?'

'And he quit. Walked out.'

'And nobody stopped him?'

'Lewis, don't –'

'Was it the temp worker?'

'It's nobody's fault.'

'Bullshit, Janice. Bull-shit. I told you –'

'Don't you dare speak to me like that. Nothing's changed, Lewis. We serve those who need it.'

'Whatever.'

'Don't do anything.'

'I'm gunna visit him. Is he down the road?'

'The Alfred. I'll sort it out… one more thing.'

He kicked a stone too hard and it crashed into the wall.

'Lewis, he's not… he's not our Dev anymore.'

He didn't respond. Fuck her. Her kids went to the same schools as mates from uni. She wasn't of this world. He had family who'd flushed their jobs, houses, marriages and sanity down the pokies, at the pub and on the streets. She was a pretender. A fucking do-gooder down here to make herself feel better about her privileged fucking life. She'd actually said – he'd overheard a conversation – that she'd rather donate her time to this place than give money to people on the street. Always on your terms, Jan. And now Devon was outside her rose-coloured glasses. There's a word for people like her.

'People don't change, Lewis.'

He walked away, leaving his bowl half-eaten on the table.

* * *

It was a grimy Melbourne day but he didn't take the tram. For a week he'd put the visit off for no reason he thought too hard about. He couldn't shake the feeling that he should've seen this coming. He bought a packet of cigarettes. The taste was trash and, because he was walking and unpracticed, he couldn't find the rhythms of when to drag or blow out.

Devon was the person he bragged about to drunken girls at parties, argued to people who questioned why he bothered volunteering, and reminded himself of when depressed. The day Lewis never forgot was when the film crew interviewed Devon. Lewis had been sitting outside in the sunny court-yard, amongst the regulars eating their lunches, while questionable wafts of smoke blew in from the mob in the alleyway. Dev's goofy smile was wider than usual and Lewis asked if he was too famous to help peel potatoes.

'Now, now, you aren't getting jealous are you? Because they didn't pick you?'

'Just thank me at the Oscars and I'll find a way to live.'

The cameras set and the lady with the microphone approached. She asked him about his job.

'I really like working at the kitchen; I volunteer five days a week from seven thirty am to three pm. I don't have any other jobs. They asked me if I wanted to get paid but I said no. Money doesn't really interest me.'

The interviewer sought out details of the fall.

Devon eyed his shifting feet. 'I haven't lived a good life. Devon doesn't have a happy story. A lot of alcohol and gambling.'

The interviewer's mouth formed a wordless shape. But Devon grinned.

'But that is over now. I've been working here three years. Lewis is my favourite. He makes everyone happy. Devon found happiness. No, no, from now on, it's all uphill from here.'

It's all uphill from here

Asserted into the camera like a universal truth.

It's all uphill from here.

It's redemption. How people can change. Belief. And that's so powerful.

* * *

'Who are you here to see?'

'Devon McBride.'

The door clicked, opened. The nurse didn't introduce herself, just ambled down the hall. It was more domestic than the movies. Instead of white walls and that sick sterile feeling – dark blue carpet, faux-wood grained walls.

In the lounge room, the worn-out nurse said, 'There you go.'

He scanned the room: a middle-aged guy with a twitch, a toothless man with a Merv Hughes mo and an old dribbling woman. They erupted like a Mexican wave, pouring out key-life moments until the nurse told them to shut up, that it was Devon's friend. Yeah, that was like the movies.

And then Dev. Were the nurses responsible for pulling the cap so ridiculously off centre? Like they wanted you to know that he'd completely lost his shit?

It's all uphill from here.

It took a moment for Dev to click and eventually he stood up. Lewis hugged him tight and told himself that Dev's limp body wasn't awkward. They sat in a corner by a window. Silence and head nods. He chastised the uneasy feeling, the creeping judgments. 'Anyway, mate, what're you doing in here?'

Many digressions followed, but also a coherent narrative. Shortly after quitting work at the kitchen, unhappy with criticisms, Devon had devoted himself to his art. Struck by the power of explosive insights, he realised that his ideas might have legs. Devon recognised that he was put on Earth to help restore eternal peace. All he needed now was the spotlight. The president of the United States was his preferred audience, but that was unrealistic. A more viable alternative was to run to Canberra with his letter and personally deliver the key to world peace direct to the prime minister. Just before he was set to leave on his mighty run, Devon thought he'd stop in at the kitchen and asked someone to deliver a message. At a less than satisfactory response, Devon threatened to kill the secretary.

'Aw, Dev. That's not very nice, mate.'

'She was rude.'

'Yeah, yeah. No, you're right.'

Conversation dragged. Lewis kept bringing it back to football but he couldn't find any momentum. Devon hunched over his folded arms and wouldn't look him in the eye. Guarding himself?

Quiet. 'So...' Lewis ran his hands through his hair, 'When are we getting you back to work?'

'Not going back.'

'Okay... then what are you going to do? What's the plan?'

'Still have to deliver my letter to the prime minister.'

'And then you can come back to work?'

'I said no,' he banged the table.

His eyes were red. Lewis mentally prepared to leave. He coughed and turned to stand, thinking of a circuit breaker. He looked back to Devon, who was grinning. Wickedly. Almost like he'd won something over Lewis. 'You said it was all uphill from here,' Lewis said.

'What?'

'You said, that it was all uphill from here. That it was all going to be alright, remember?'

Devon tilted his head.

'You reckon you don't need work? Look where you are, for God's sake.'

'Be quiet.'

'You said this had finished and –'

'Shut-up.'

'You're pathetic. You've been down –'

'Go away.' Devon's face shuddered. 'Go away or I will kill you.' Both fists were clenched on the table.

The nurse found a bit of purpose. Kicked Lewis out. He wasn't welcome back.

Lewis couldn't afford to go to the pub and wanted to be alone, so he bought a flask and drifted over to the park across the road where he sat on a pile of dead oak leaves. After a few slugs, the cigarettes weren't so bad. Under big trees or park benches and green patches, the growing homeless clustered around their trolleys and tents, passing paper-bagged bottles. After he'd given one cigarette away, word got out and the packet disappeared. Until working at the kitchen, he'd understood how fragile the distinction was between being a customer and not being one.

It's all uphill from here.

He imagined Sisyphus pushing the rock up the hill. Had Devon misunderstood something? Or had James?

Either way, it was cold and getting darker.

24

Suburban Graveyard

Victor Chrisnaa Senthinathan

HIGHEST-PLACING MONASH UNIVERSITY STUDENT IN THE MONASH PRIZE

Graveyards were running out of space for the dead, according to my dad who was currently reading the newspaper. The increasing population meant there had never been more people dying in Australia than at this moment, and our golden soil couldn't keep up with the exponentially increasing demand. Cemeteries were limited by the urban sprawl of the cities and had no room to grow into. This looming crisis of where to inter our breathless, tombless bodies had however been buried in the papers by concerns over global warming and the economy and immigration.

The synagogues and the mosques and the churches had realised the earth was not big enough to hide the dead, and were starting to panic, according to the newspaper column. Would we be forced to place them on top of each other like shipping containers? Would we be forcing the dead to pay rent? Would we be hauling their bodies out of the pockmarked earth if they fell behind on their repayment schedules?

This sense of alarm very much appealed to my dad, a man with entrepreneurial spirit but no ideas worthy of that entrepreneurial spirit. He was constantly searching for the right business venture that would allow him to quit his thankless accounting job. He would read the newspapers every evening after coming back from work, gnawing on mango slices as he searched for inspiration. This impending graveyard crisis, which was still unknown enough for my dad to have no competition when devising a business strategy, was a stroke of luck that my dad was determined to capitalise on.

'We can lease our backyard and make it a graveyard,' my dad said as he skinned another mango. 'The government will pay us for the space. We could create a business helping lease other people's backyards until these white people learn about cremation.' My dad's eyes were already shining with finder's fees and corporations and tax numbers. 'What do you think?' he asked, looking at me.

'What about hot air balloons?' I said, trying to contribute to this imagined macabre business empire trading on future corpses. 'Balloons in the sky with floating coffins underneath. You wouldn't run out of space then, in the air,' I said, imagining the fleet of balloons exhaling helium, drifting through the sky, coffins gently swaying underneath like wooden kites. Sponsors could fight for room on the billowing fabric of the balloons. The balloons could float around Australia, a juxtaposition of joy and death serving as a poignant reminder of our mortality.

'Don't be ridiculous,' my dad said, not even sparing me a disdainful glance as he started cutting the graveyard article out of the paper, the sinewy slabs of mango on his plate forgotten. 'Who would want their grandma floating behind their house?'

* * *

My parents sat on the veranda a week later, drinking coconut water and staring out at our former backyard, which had played host to banana yellow excavators with growling stomachs. The council had knocked down the wall and windows of our house that faced east for easier access to the backyard (after assuring my dad there would be appropriate compensation, as well as a shiny plaque on the replacement wall commemorating our communal spirit).

Our backyard was unrecognisable now with the government having dug the graves incredibly close to each other. The craters were arrayed in a hatched pattern, empty plots in a grid now waiting for families to pay for the privilege of burying their loved ones.

My dad was pointing at specific holes now, with dirt heaped next to them, and saying who would be buried where, while my mum laughed.

1   Hole at the middle of the fence: James, my dad's first boss in
      Australia, who was a fan of racial abuse or mild banter depending
      on your perspective, and who cycled through calling my dad a taxi
      driver/telemarketer/janitor

2   Hole at the centre of the backyard: Rajesh, a family friend who was
      prone to jealousy. My mum swore that he had placed the evil eye
      on me when I was a teenager, subsequently leading to all my future
      problems

3   Hole that was in front of our (former) window: Vikram the blind,
      who was not actually blind but merely drove like he was. My dad's
      insurance premiums went up after an unfortunate rear-ending
      incident.

'How do you know who's going where?' I asked after a lull in their conversation. 'And why do they all know us?'

'I don't know who's going where,' my dad said. 'Now, how would you
feel if Dave was under there?' He pointed to one hole near the centre of the
fence, next to James's future plot, where the tree that my dad and I had used
as a makeshift stump when playing cricket in my childhood used to stand. It
was a young fragile thing, a thin trunk with dewy green leaves. I was always
scared of it being uprooted when I batted. And now it was gone to make
room for a dead body.

Dave was our neighbour and had lived a house down my whole life. The
ornery man had earned our lifelong enmity by refusing to throw back the
tennis balls my dad had willowed over the fence for six.

'I don't know,' I said. 'Dave's not even dead, Dad. Why is he getting
buried in the first place?'

'It's not about being dead, it's not about the buried. This is about imagination, it's about picturing your problems and then burying them, out of sight
so they don't annoy you,' my dad said, shaking the bottle so the last drops of
coconut water would splay out to his tongue.

My mum held up a purple book. 'The Dalai Lama wrote about it. You can
also pretend your problems are leaves on the water and then –'

'The problem is that you have no imagination,' my dad continued over my
mum, tilting the bottle back to get the last few drops of water. 'You just wait
for things to change and you hope that things will turn out alright. But life
does not work like that.'

We were silent then, listening to the cawing magpies with their skinny feet furrowing the earth. 'Why haven't we leased the space under the veranda yet?' my dad asked my mum as he got up, throwing the water bottle onto the graveyard for the contractors to clean up, leaving me and my mum behind.

* * *

A month later, almost all the plots available had been bought at exorbitant prices. Bodies were placed underneath the earth, their tombstones jutting out like cloud grey seashells on the beach. The tessellating tumuli had formed fleshy brown waves crashing onto the fences. The veranda had been demolished and replaced by a row of enamel plaques. Only one plot remained unsold: the one in the corner where my mum would stand at square leg when we played cricket.

That night, the air was damp and hot. My shirt clung to my chest and the air was burning my skin and the fan wasn't working. I got out of my bed and tried walking around the room, hoping it would cool me down. When I looked out the windows at the graveyard –

Perched on the gravestones were languid ghosts, stardust skin and pale moon eyes, ethereal butterfly wings floating in the backyard with voices that fell like raindrops. They looked at me but from so far away I could not see their faces. Maybe it was Dave and James and Ramesh sliding over the marble.

The ghosts started jumping in and out into the last available plot, treating the pool of darkness like a trampoline, their bodies tangling and blurring together into a haze of glitter.

Then Ramesh saw my silhouette on the window and started waving his hand with a slow carelessness. 'Join us,' he whispered, and his voice was beautiful like grass-scented rain sliding down a car window. I felt like opening the window and tumbling to the ground, gambolling with the spirits away from living eyes under the stars.

Then there was a noise from behind me, from behind my bedroom door. It was the snore of my dad, the rattling sound of a lawnmower trying to start underwater that had haunted my nights since childhood. I turned around, surprised, and when I turned back, Ramesh had turned away from me. He jumped into the empty tomb and in the sparkling fog composed of so many spirits, I could not tell when he had reappeared.

I stood there, behind the window, watching the ghosts dance until dawn when the sun rose into a sky that had been coloured the purple of bruised skin and the ghosts evaporated into nothingness.

* * *

When I went to the dining room for breakfast that morning, my dad was cutting out another article from the newspaper. My mum was sucking on the pulp of a mango.

'Have you heard about trust falls?' my dad asked. 'I'm reading about it now. It is a synergistic way of building trust in a team-orientated environment.' The last bit was read out stiltedly from the newspaper, my dad sounding out the syllables of synergistic.

'What is that?' my mum asked, her teeth stained with mango juice.

'He means it's an exercise for trust,' I said.

'Yes, it is for us to learn how to depend on each other. I think it might be good for us to do. We've been growing apart and it's important for families to stick together.'

'Sure,' I said. 'Now?'

'Yes, now. Let's use the empty hole outside,' my dad said.

'Why can't we just do it here on actual ground where it's safe?' I said, looking at my dad who was looking away from me and at the news article.

'Because, we need consequences, actual real-life consequences,' my dad said. 'You wouldn't care otherwise. We need to show that we trust each other.' My dad nodded to himself before walking outside, expecting us to follow.

The empty grave was hidden in the shadows cast by the fence. My parents and I stood on opposite sides of the grave lengthwise, with me being squished between the edge of the grave and the fence. My parents stood on the other side, their shadows falling away from the grave.

'Are you sure this hole isn't too long?' I asked, peering down into the impenetrable blackness. I couldn't see where the bottom of the grave was.

'Don't you trust us?' my dad asked, hurt in his voice. I turned around, my hands scrabbling on the top of the fence for purchase.

I took a deep breath. I let go of the fence.

I   fall

                                        fall

                                            fall

And we had miscalculated, or at least I had miscalculated, because the grave was just slightly longer than my body. It all happened so quick in the space of an inhale, so quick everything had blurred together and I couldn't see as I fell down where my dad's arms were, whether it was the wind or my dad's hands that grabbed at my hair, whether it was the howl of the wind or the howl of my mum that was in my ears as I disappeared.

My shoulders scraped against the dirt walls and the shadows squeezed around my body in a straitjacket and my scream disappeared into the emptiness that surrounded me I was a blurred fugue my limbs pushed back into my body my breath torn from my throat my eyes macerated by the wind the corporality of my body lost to silence. The earth had swallowed me.

And the souls of the people who had invited me did not appear so far underground as to give me company.

25

Dervishes

Pip Griffin

Last night I watched dervishes whirl
skirts white arcs
heads inclined in precarious cone hats
arms exquisitely positioned
faces composed in ritual rapture
a spectacle of male mystery.

One – black-cloaked
not whirling
moved artfully amongst them
like a mummer.

Their dancing
rather than revealing a transcendence
conjured a forbidden world
and latent fear
whirl-pooled from pages
of a childhood picture book.

26

Kaimanawa Horses

Jackson C. Payne

I saw them once. On the Desert Road. Mount Ruapehu was holding up the clouds like a table leg. Dad was turning the dial on the car stereo while Mum drove, the road rising and falling in front of us as we sped into the deep blue end of the day. I looked out my window and there they were, galloping along the side of the road in the nearly dark. A huge silver stallion was at the head, its nose down, its mane and tail like fire in the wind. There were maybe twenty of them but they all ran as one. Steam rose from their bodies and it reminded me of photos I'd seen of comets in space. I read once that the haze around a comet is called a coma, dust and gas from the Sun's radiation. That's what they were.

'Denis, just leave it,' said Mum. 'There's no reception out here.'

'Will you just let me check. Bloody hell.'

I wanted to say to them, *Look, horses. Wild horses. Kaimanawa horses.* But they wouldn't have understood.

The horses heaved with the rhythm of their hooves against the dirt, moving over the tussock as if that was the only thing to be doing. The silver one turned its head to me without slowing, its eyes a black I'd never known. It was too much so I turned away, only for only a second, but when I looked back they were gone.

I was on my back on the floor of my room reading when Mum and Dad knocked. They sat on the edge of my bed, the closest to each other I'd seen them in a long time. They had on their faces they used when we went to see Nana in the rest home. Mum looked at Dad in a way that said *Go on*, but he didn't, so Mum went first.

'Son, Mrs MacIntosh called. She's worried about you. So are we.'

'She said in the classroom it's like you're there but not,' said Dad.

'We want to take you to see someone. A doctor.'

They both bent down to hug me and it was a strange feeling because they weren't huggers. I could hear their hushed voices after they closed the door, spitting words at each other as they went up the hall.

The doctor didn't know what to do so he sent me to a psychologist. She didn't know what was wrong so she sent me to a psychiatrist. At Braemar Hospital. A girl in my class did her history project on the place and said it used to be called the Nelson Lunatic Asylum. It was right across the street from my school and was part of its vocabulary. If someone was acting crazy you said, *Fuck off to Braemar, retard.* Or just, *Hey Braemar.*

'This is silly, why can't I park there?' said Mum, pointing to a park outside school.

'Mum, please! They'll see.'

She drove around the corner and braked abruptly.

'Mum, am I a lunatic?'

'What? Who said that?'

'Don't worry.'

I got out of the car before she could ask any more questions.

Whitewashed walls stunk of disinfectant, made my eyes water. A lady at reception wearing horn-rimmed glasses with a gold chain attached to the arms looked at me like I was crazy when I asked her where Dr Eastbourne's office was. She didn't say a word but raised her crooked index finger that pointed both down the corridor and back from where I had come. I followed the hall.

I found the door with his name on it, hand-painted on frosted glass. I knocked. There was a long pause before he called me in. His desk had on it a pile of folders so high I could only just meet his magnified eyes. Beyond his desk, in the window, was a fenced paddock in which three horses, their noses to the ground, ripped at the grass.

In the olden days escaped horses from sheep stations roamed the plains, before the Desert Road cut through the guts, before military men drove their tanks through the tussock firing blank rounds in mock war, before holidaymakers made their way to the snow for fun. Equine refugees stomping over the tundra, lost, until finally there they were. The rest. And they ran and they ate and they fought and they fucked

until their numbers were in the thousands, no longer stateless beasts but owners of
the ranges and ridges and hills of the Kaimanawas, the Kaimanawa Horses.

The pills made my mouth a desert, the walls puffy, and I always needed to lie down. When people spoke, it was as if they were far away. Everything tasted like metal, even water. Especially water.

On my second visit to Dr Eastbourne, Mum pulled up directly opposite school where the blue and grey uniforms swarmed the hill.

'What are you doing?'

'What does it look like?'

'Not here. 'Round the corner.'

'Don't be silly. It's time you stopped being ashamed of yourself.'

'I'm not getting out.'

'If you don't get out I'll honk the horn and shout your name.'

'You'd never.'

The horn squawked. She started winding down her window.

'Alright, alright.'

I slammed the door and moved away as fast as I could. She tooted and the tyres screeched on the road.

Dr Eastbourne was exactly as I'd found him the week before, only the pile of folders now completely hid him. I took a seat on a plastic chair in front of his desk and watched the horses through the window. A chestnut-coloured foal and a mare were nuzzling each other. A trainer was trying to wrestle a bit into the mouth of a large black stallion but he was having none of it. He kept flicking his head and whinnying. Dr Eastbourne looked at me, surprised, as if seeing me for the first time.

'How are you feeling?'

'Good.'

'And the pills?'

'Alright, I guess.'

'Great. Are they making you hungrier?'

'No.'

'Then I'll up your dose.'

The school grounds were naked but for some left-behind balls and school jumpers orphaned in the grass. Inside I handed Mrs MacIntosh the note Mum gave me, the one that said I had an *appointment* without, thank God, saying exactly where I'd been. She read it over her glasses and without moving her head looked up at me.

'Take a seat.'

I took the only spare desk – in the middle of the class. A kid behind me started sniggering.

'Is something funny, Mr Thorne?' Mrs MacIntosh asked.

'No, miss.'

It was David Thorne. They said his dad was an All Black.

Then came the farms. At first they were few and they were small but soon they grew to meet the needs of a growing country, multiplying miles of land the Kaimanawa Horses once had to themselves. Now confined to a narrow strip near the ranges without food, they died off in large numbers. Again refugees, skinny, their coats ragged or coming out in clumps, they tallied just a few hundred and plodded weakly in search of what? Finding only angry bullets from fearful farmers. But some politicians in the capital huffed and puffed like the wind there, building a storm of popular opinion until the Kaimanawa Horses became protected.

Mum and Dad moved around each other in the kitchen with the distance of container ships at sea. But it wasn't far enough. Cupboards and drawers argued with each other as they opened and closed, knives came down and echoed like slammed doors.

'Will you get out of the way?' said Dad, straining spaghetti in the sink.

'I'm not eating spag' bol' again.'

'Sort your own dinner out then.'

'Can't you see that's what I'm doing?'

Dad had lost his job a few years before so he did most of the house stuff, cleaning and laundry, that sort of thing. Only, Mum hated his cooking.

'We'll talk about this later,' said Mum under her breath, ripping the arms off some broccoli.

Dad put down a bowl of pasta in front of me. The sauce had the consistency of water and the spaghetti was all stuck together. I wanted what Mum was having even though it was raw vegetables. But really, I didn't care. The pills had created in me a senseless hunger. I would eat until I felt sick and ten minutes later I would again be hungry.

'So, I've got some exciting news,' said Mum, sitting down at the table. 'I've got a new job. With New Zealand Thoroughbred Racing.'

'News to me,' said Dad.

'Only bloody found out today.'

Her eyes cut through him. My knife screamed against my plate.

'What will you be doing, Mum?'

'There was a bit of a problem with the government last year with, well, doping. So they've brought me in to manage that.'

'You'll be good at that,' I said.

We sat in hungry silence, Mum and Dad's disgruntled eating the only sound in the room. Despite my hunger I couldn't stay there being eaten by their resentment. I excused myself.

'Where do you think you're going? Pills first,' Mum said.

But then there were just way too many of them. Or so they said. Government protection meant Kaimanawa Horses had run freely over the ranges for decades. But the same suits who protected them saw the Kaimanawas as a risk to something more important: Plants. So the helicopters went up and fences were built and men with dirt and blood in the cracks of their palms took guns from their cupboards they'd been wanting to use for oh so long but finally the government had seen some fucking sense as to what those bastard horses were doing.

Dr Eastbourne's office was next to a locked door. The glass on the door was frosted but in it were scrapes, like those from fingernails.

On my third visit he had in his office a murmuration of doctors. I could hear them through the door.

'She's taking the maximum dose.'

'Let's try her on something else. Something stronger.'

'Yes, yes, okay.'

Their eyes diagnosed me as they filed out and toward the door. They quickly unlocked it and squeezed through, echoed footsteps down the corridor becoming quiet as they moved away. Then I heard it. That beautiful scream. It swirled around me, through me, the ends of my nerves fizzing with feeling as if for the first time.

I left.

I walked down the corridor, through the automatic doors, crossed the road from the hospital and up the front path to school. David Thorne stood with his arms crossed, smiling through his blonde regrowth that hung in ringlets down his forehead.

'What's it like living at Braemar, retard?'

I saw on television footage shot from helicopters. Kaimanawa horses ran in long chains with such force that I finally knew the meaning of the word horsepower. I looked for him. I wanted to see those deep black eyes and I wanted to know if he was as big as he was in my mind. There was always a different string of horses led by a stallion that was black or brown or white but never silver. Never him. And I was glad. Those horses all ended up in pens and taken in trucks to the slaughterhouse where they were slit and skinned and minced for dog food.

'Hurry up, take your pills. We're late.'

Mum watched as I put them in my mouth and swallowed.

'Just need to get something from my room,' I said.

'I'll be in the car.'

I ran down the hall and into my room, pulled back my bottom drawer, took the pill from beneath my tongue and put it in the old jam jar with the rest. They were partly dissolved from my spit and looked insane. I don't know why I didn't just throw them away; for some reason I couldn't.

But everything had stopped tasting like metal.

She was revving the car impatiently when Dad and I stepped onto the back porch, her hands fixed to the steering wheel as though the car was already in motion. Dad struggled with his tie; his shirt was untucked at the back.

'Come on, Denis. Chrissake. You might be happy in the cushy world of unemployment but I'm sure as hell not.'

'What's that supposed to mean?'

'It means if you embarrass me in front of my new boss we'll all be eating two-minute noodles. Tuck in your shirt and get in.'

Cars of all colours in perfect rows like mismatched Lego. Men in bright orange vests waved us through the not-quite-shorn grass to an empty spot in the corner. The women wore misshapen hats, some with fake fruit attached; the men in suits they hadn't worn since the last family funeral. They all walked cautiously over the grass, sure to not stand in sheep shit as they made their way to the stands, to bubbly in plastic cups and the smell of frying hot dogs in the breeze. Not us. We were in the corporate box, Mum's first chance to schmooze.

'Stop,' she said.

She licked her thumb and rubbed spit in the corner of Dad's mouth where an old bit of food must have dried, fixed his tie and smoothed over his hair. She looked at me, smiled.

'Come on.'

So many men, all in black or navy with shoes the colour of oil; wives clustered in a gaggle at the snacks table regarding each other stiffly, picking and pecking at food in between their spluttering laughter. Mum edged in with the men, next to one with a full head of white hair, and soon their attention was on her as she told a joke about some politician she knew in Wellington.

The racetrack was framed by a rectangular glass wall. Trainers in red and black led horses around a small enclosure as men with fists full of ticket stubs leaned against the railing.

Dad and I took plastic plates of finger food and sat on the deck to watch the first race. The horses frothed and flicked as the jockeys in bright satin forced them into the starting gate. The horses' eyes flashed white and dangerous. The starting gun sounded and hooves sent great wads of dirt in the air as they took off, beyond the first bend and further than we could see. The announcer's words galloped and beat through a buzzing speaker and soon the horses were coming back around the home straight in a long line but their manes were plaited and their tales were trimmed and they did not gallop as one.

The back of Mrs MacIntosh's arm sploshed like water in a bottle as she wrote on the board. David Thorne walked in and smiled at me, walked to the person sitting behind me and tapped him on the shoulder. The boy got up and moved without a word.

David whispered it close, his breath hot on my ear.

'Braemar.'

'Mr Thorne! What is so important that it can't wait until after class?'

'Sorry, Miss. I was just telling him to be quiet. He keeps trying to tell me about his weekend.'

She frowned, said nothing, turned back to the board and continued writing. David laughed behind me but it was as if I wasn't there.

Mum and Dad were arguing in the dining room. Something about money. Always money. I wanted to listen but there he was, on the television, the silver stallion. I moved closer and turned it up but something was wrong. He wasn't galloping over the Kaimanawas, he was alone in a pen, his wild eyes searching for his drove but they were gone. A small helicopter flew above another group of horses, driving them from the ranges and into fields that had been fenced off. The reporter said the number of horses was too high, that the government was moving in to do a kill. No, a cull. They would be taken to a meatworks to be turned into dog food.

I turned off the television and left the lounge, past my parents whose voices had become louder.

'You always do this, Denis. Just grow up will you.'

'Jesus. Listen to yourself.'

I closed the door to my room and took from beneath my drawer the jam jar of half-dissolved pills. I tipped them into my hand, put my hand to my mouth and once again tasted metal.

27

Basket Press

Ben Grech

I arrived early with a $90 bottle of Basket Press Shiraz and a rented blazer. We were celebrating the end of our undergrads, our future successes, my scholarship to McGill. Dave and Stacy owned the place, a small terrace house in Fitzroy, the first of us to own anything. Stacy was older, had left University, and was already working as an Engineer. None of us were surprised that Dave landed Stacy.

I approached the gate and thought about how each weekend I'd walked with the group back to their college, where they'd leave me at the gate, drunk, listening to one of Dave's drunken stories fade as the group moved across the grounds, before walking the couple of kays back to my share house in Collingwood.

Dave poured a round of whiskey. Stacy said maybe we should take it slow and I said tonight wasn't about going slow.

'Hear, hear,' said Dave, who agreed that I could handle it, and clinked my glass.

'Don't worry,' Stacy said when I asked who was coming. 'Alice is on her way.'

Sasha arrived next, jeans and t-shirt and a heavy faux gold chain, looking more glamorous than any of us. She took a glass of wine and sat next to me at the counter. She kissed me on the cheek.

'Long time,' she said.

'To the future,' I said, and lifted my glass.

Becky burst through the door and shouted 'what up bitches' wearing a pantsuit and a pair of Adidas shell toes. Dave poured her the last glass of wine and said compliments of Moggy over here. She raised her glass and downed it.

I've always hated the name Moggy. I tried to take on Morgan when I started Uni but Dave called me Moggy and it stuck. It makes me think of a boy, almost well liked, always just out of reach of popularity, hiding his insecurities behind indifference and frustration. *Nice* but *goofy* and *irreverent*.

When Alice arrived I kissed her on the cheek and we lingered. She said it was lovely to see me and that it had been too long. Confidence, I thought. More push, more open, more opportunities, more luck, more pride, more acceptance. Stacy walked Alice through to the lounge and when Dave passed he gave me a wink.

Dave was brilliant. An overachiever. He won the awards, the scholarships, when we went to the best parties, it was because he invited us. He was close friends with Dicky O'Brien, who'd already had two plays at the Malthouse and a session at the Wheeler Centre. I'd even heard rumours Dave had slept with Katy Cartwright, that actress from *Home and Away*. And he'd landed Stacy.

We sat around on cushions and shared our plans. Sasha, an internship at ABC, which we nodded at, only half mockingly; Becky was moving to New York to 'see what was out there' and while we publicly commended her bravery, privately, we knew this was code for 'couldn't land a job.' Dave, coddling with Stacy, completing his articles at Baker and McKinley; Brian, something to do with trading at his father's firm; Alice, an assistant advisory position to the local Labor member.

I didn't mention my application for an on-line editor position at *Six Feet of Fiction* that went unreturned. Or my rejected short story *The Meadow Over Hill*, which I'd sent out to several magazines. I was learning to accept failure gracefully as a step towards success, and that meant not complaining. It meant riding the wave and taking the tide.

As the night went on, the walls breathing with our fate, pate and cheeses and Pinot, we asked each other 'future questions.' Where are you going to live? What kind of car are you going to drive? Who are you going to marry? We were the kind of drunk that feels magic. No matter how much we put away, we were witty and charming and intelligent beyond our years.

Alice reached across and slid her fingers between mine. Any other night, I would have been surprised. But with our potentials in reach, having already – in our minds – surpassed our unsupportive parents, our dismissive high school teachers, that one Professor in second year who had it out for us, nothing was out of the question. I stroked the ridge of Alice's knuckle and felt confident and excited and sure that this was the beginning of something special.

'Who's got another question?' someone, it might have been me, shouted. There was stuttering and silence and from Brian, who'd said it innocently enough, came 'what's your deepest fear?' We oohd and ahhed at that. But the room had changed. I felt the drink settle. My hand felt sweaty and uncomfortable and Alice pulled away. The answers were mostly silly. Dying young, not finding love, settling too early. When it came back to Brian he said, 'Regret. I'm afraid of looking back and regretting my life.' It was silly. Someone threw a cushion, I think. But it stuck. Like a curse.

The evening quieted. A breeze rushed through and Dave kicked the door free from the flowerpot holding it open. We spoke sparingly, people finished their wine, spoke about the week. When Sasha spilled the last of her wine over the table, we used it as an excuse to leave. At home I would notice the dark stain on my blazer and have to purchase it from the rentals.

We kissed goodbye and wished each other luck and promised to do this again every month. I asked Alice if she'd like to walk home and she nodded and smiled. I turned and watched Dave and Stacy, arms linked, not knowing that they'd get married, and divorced, within the next five years. Not knowing the phrase 'at least they didn't have kids,' would get so overused in conversations about their separation that it would cease to mean anything.

Over the years, my Master's slipped into a PhD, which is now three years and two supervisors overdue. My teaching career adds up to three semesters of part time work and a handful of relief days at a dozen or so of the worst schools across the state.

When living in Montreal for my scholarship, I took a trip to New York and met with Becky. I remembered her fragile hope during that dinner party about finding 'something'. She'd landed a job at a good publishing company and her life, it seemed to me, was set. After this I got blind drunk and slept with a girl who lived above a bookstore. She wasn't a big reader and I couldn't help thinking it was such a waste. I was dating someone in Montreal at the time. It was serious, but even then, in my mid-twenties, I thought serious came and went. I told her about the girl above the bookstore and she left. I haven't dated anyone longer than a few weeks since.

When Alice and I walked home that night, as we approached her place, her wearing my jacket, both her hands curled around my arm, I asked her if she was thinking about Brian's response. About fearing regret. It didn't faze her, she said. 'What good is a life without any regret?' I would find out years later that she and Dave had been having an affair and that they had fucked that night in the bathroom after dinner. She lost an earring in the sink. We talked a little but the spark had gone. She kissed me goodnight, on the cheek, whispered that she'd never liked the name Moggy, thought Morgan suited me better, and left me on the sidewalk.

28

Obsessive Compulsive

Carolyn Gerrish

1. Security Magic

Can we ever be safe?   hand hiding keypad
protects your identity   & before leaving the house
ensure your birth certificate passport   credit cards
are in the desk drawer then use the deadlock
spare key secreted in the hole between the bricks
tap ten times on the spyhole   but return before
you've even gone touch wood your home is still
standing the door **was** locked the iron gas & taps
turned off could this intemperate checking regime
appease the gods of menace

                        never harm

                                    nor spell
                                        nor charm

& when at the theatre   fingers crossed the least
dangerous place to be   is near the exit if there's
a fire or terrorist attack   you'll be first out on the road
safe as houses & when dining with friends   always
occupy the same seat   for that is where your safety sits
but if you're still on the street after dark   for sure

a vampire will carry you off & eliminate thirteen
from your calculations   skip past it with confidence
fourteen is much better equipped to fight off threats

but those ritual-mongers the Aztecs   feared
without human sacrifice   the sun would go
on strike   lose its heat   fall away in a flaccid
heap

at McDonald's plenty of dining places   but he needs
to establish an arcane order to avert disaster
stands near the window   meticulously plants
his fast food along the sill   frozen coke big mac
choc chip cookies   hotcakes   standing firm as a
row of judges

2. *Footpath Ritual*

see the secret smile
on the face of the pacer
as she walks back & forth
back & forth –
how many more steps
before her race is complete
won't count the cost
so little reward
such a need to hurry –
but while she's high
on movement
she can't stop
& worry

29

Sweet Chariot

Jane Downing

'Do you think Bright is called Bright because of the brightness of the light?'

The two women, side by side, stared out over the glistening, rushing river that made Bright such a lovely place to visit. Maureen rolled her eyes at Betty's question, but not so emphatically that Betty would notice. Betty was being overly bright with her enthusiasms, but death did that to some people. Funerals are a time of platitudes and banalities.

Neither really knew the daughter of their deceased friend. She'd been friendly enough when they arrived and was being stoic at the picnic table since they'd wandered en masse over to the river. She looked like someone who'd be more comfortable in a traditional funeral home under the charge of a traditional funeral director and the influence of traditional funereal music. (A Bruno Mars hit filtered over from a group of loose-limbed adolescents further along the river bank.) The daughter's hair was drawn tightly from her face and her clothes were navy, fitted and coordinated. Maureen and Betty had earlier agreed there was nothing of her (poor dead) mother in her.

Her mother, Lilith, had loved Bright. There were memories here – unspecified, hinted at, happy, dramatic, or at the very least, lasting memories – in this small High Country town of European trees and rushing river. Lilith had made it to ninety. Longevity is genetic and a fine legacy. Her daughter had no choice but to fulfil Lilith's last wish: 'Cast my ashes upon the Ovens.'

It was generally agreed that Lilith had kept her marbles to the end. Longevity and lucidity: life's lottery won. Nevertheless, the daughter (apparently) threw her hands around in confusion upon hearing the wish and addressed the nurse. 'But it was my father's family who lost everyone in the ovens. Mum and her lot came out well before the war.'

Maureen had arrived to visit her dying friend in the Melbourne hospice so was eyewitness to the rest, which she'd confided to Betty over a wine the same night. To wit, Lilith raising her croaking, dying voice above the hubbub to clarify, 'The Ovens is a river. In Bright. In the High Country.'

Betty had observed, that same sad evening, three wines in, political correctness a distant concept, 'Just as well. My pension wouldn't stretch to a funeral in Dachau.'

Maureen, in her most morose voice, had told her not to be so morbid. And Betty obviously remembered the chastisement, hence her gratingly buoyant tone by the river at their dear friend's send-off. By the Ovens river.

* * *

'What's her name again?' Betty asked Maureen in an unfortunate stage whisper at the picnic funeral.

They turned like synchronised swimmers to look over at their friend's daughter who had her head down, unpacking things and thingamabobs out onto the greying wood table.

Maureen couldn't remember the daughter's name either. Lilith hadn't talked about her much during their long friendship. So Maureen shrugged and drew her white Jackie Onassis sunglasses down off her head to shade her eyes. For the light was indeed bright. The sunglasses did not become Maureen – and she did not pretend they did; but sunglasses cost so much and she'd remembered these 1950s originals in the back of her drawer when her last lot had recently been crushed under a wheel of her son's Honda.

Betty squinted at her own reflection in her friend's sunglasses, her question unanswered as she'd assumed the shrug was aimed at the hovering flies. She did not like her reflection and turned her back on the river completely and watched the performance over their mutual friend's urn. Which was just one of the many unpacked items on the wooden outdoor table.

These two old self-described ducks (the river had feathered ducks too) were, despite their age, a little naïve about death. They were both equally surprised that the urn on the picnic table was not Ming china, or hand-thrown pottery, or patterned in gold, or in any way attractive. It looked like an esky; something in the duck-egg blue plastic suggested this comparison strongly. The daughter picked this travesty up to carry to the river. By the way the daughter carried it – in front, two arms cradling it away from her navy jacket – this receptacle was weighty.

Lilith had been such a tiny thing under the sheets at the end, when she'd asked to be cast upon the Ovens.

The funeral group was mustered by the movement, coming from various points in the riverside park, sheep reconvening as a flock. At last, some ritual to relieve them of the enormity of thinking about death. They stood in a semicircle by the river, Lilith's family and friends, eleven in all, almost as many as at the Last Supper.

Maureen was the only one in black. There were shades of grey amongst the others gathered, while Betty, working on the premise that Lilith had never been sombre in life, so why force it on her now, was a rainbow of colour. More psychedelic hippy, though, than God's promise to mankind. Purple shirt, red trousers, orange woolly jumper and a floral gypsy shawl against any breeze that might spring up. Maureen had to push her out-of-date sunglasses further back on her nose when she contemplated her.

The daughter, meanwhile, stuck a fingernail under the stopper of the esky (which they would only later call 'the urn' because its appearance had not yet earned the name). Nothing shifted. The gathered friends turned to each other, their eyes politely diverted from this stalling to the expected solemn rite. They made small talk to give the woman private space in which to retrieve her mother. Maureen glanced back at her. The face of the woman whose name escaped her, was screwed up in exertion and frustration.

The daughter simply could not get the stopper off life's final esky. Her nails were false (for whose nails are so perfectly edged and red?) but they were not to blame. Her husband's big, blunt hands were equally useless. The daughter's daughter had a go – young people are recognised to have ways and means. Yet the stopper securing Lilith's ashes would not budge. Before friends felt compelled to have a go, the husband's man-brain kicked in and he remembered the tools in his boot. His screwdriver was sent for. Finally, the youngest grandchild became animated behind his dark fringe and loped off through the park beside the river. Maureen watched. He was soon beside the toilet block, heading in the direction of the car park.

Without liturgy, or any movement at all, there was silence. Maureen feared Betty was going to fill this silence. Betty's lipstick mouth was wider than her real mouth and looked poised to speak.

Luckily the daughter was twitching in a way that suggested she too was uncomfortable with the lull in activity. Grief is an inconsiderate creature that lurks and lobs itself into such gaps.

'Champagne,' she cried. 'We can start now.'

No one disagreed.

The necessaries were fetched from the picnic table to the riverbank. Corks popped flamboyantly. This felt right. Lilith had loved champagne.

The glasses were plastic with removable stands, but at least they mimicked the shape of sophistication. The bubbles charged up, demanding release at the surface.

The underage granddaughter demanded her share. Her mother certainly had no reserves to argue.

Maureen sipped. Betty gulped and a false eyelash dived in for a swim; she fished it out as if it were a mayfly. One lash on, one lash off, she looked like she was winking.

'Here comes Jackson,' Jackson's sister spied.

The whole party turned to watch the adolescent swordfight his way down a line of poplars. He didn't know he was being observed; he was too old to be caught brandishing a screwdriver like some fictional character. In his mind he was The Doctor with a sonic screwdriver (obviously). Maureen saw Zorro. Betty saw Luke Skywalker. His mother looked away.

Betty couldn't stand the renewed silence any longer. In her stage whisper, 'The screwdriver makes a good Life Saver.'

There'd been no lives saved that night in the hospice: there'd been no Life Saver for Lilith. Nor had she died by the violence of a Light Sabre or equivalent, nor the Nazi ovens, nor misadventure, unless life is an adventure and the last step a miss.

There was no time, however, for Maureen to correct Betty's misnaming of science fiction weaponry. The screwdriver had quickly done the trick. It angled into the grove where the stopper and the esky-like container met, and with a few grunts (from the son-in-law) and a champagne-cork pop, Lilith was free. She was now ready for her last journey.

* * *

'Excuse me,' said a new and tentative voice.

The focus had been so surely on Lilith's esky that no one had seen the man approach. But there he was on the outside of their huddled, hushed circle, swaying slightly against an imagined breeze. He was old, plaid-trousered, cardigan-ed, the clothes old too. Maureen avoided looking at his crotch; he was the type of old man who'd inadvertently forget his fly, leaving a scrap of shirt poking out like a flag on a tugboat. Betty was reminded of her own father, Maureen of how old they too must look.

'Excuse me,' he croaked again, an arm raised, revealing a slow un-knitting in the fabric of his khaki cardigan. He swayed precipitously. He leant against the daughter's husband who just happened to be closest. Implicated by touch, the daughter's husband was solicitous.

'Can we help you?'

Maureen raised her sunglasses and her eyes met Betty's. All four eyes widened into strangled fish eyes. They made assumptions and silently shared them across the crisp Bright morning.

So this is why Lilith loved Bright.

So this was the past come to pay respect.

So this was the old lover.

So this was the current lover kept secret.

So this was the turning point of the funeral.

Oh Lilith would have loved to be here for this.

The whole party – if this was the right word for the participants of a grave ceremony – turned to stare at the old intruder. His eyes squinted behind thick prescription glasses and gave no indication of taking them all in.

Maureen had to strain to hear his next utterance, or mutterance.

'My mobility scooter has gone and got bogged. Any chance of giving us a hand pushing her back up to the path?'

The offending vehicle was spotted at a lean behind the next stand of trees. It looked well and truly stuck. A lot-of-effort-to-remove stuck. Maureen joined Betty in finding a picturesque view across the river and ignoring the question, in case they were seen as part of the solution.

The men of Lilith's wider family were sweaty when they got back. Their mood was lighter; doing good deeds does that to moods. The son-in-law knocked back more champagne and boomed out a jovial, 'Well let's get on with it then.'

* * *

Lilith's daughter did the honours. She clambered down the last steep descent of the Ovens' bank, now clutching the ash's esky like a rugby player going in for a try. Mud splattered up her neat trouser leg. She came to a halt, then sank a little, before finding a flat stone to stand on. Her shoes looked like they may have to be thrown out. She looked at them, and then back up at the audience on the bank. She searched for words, failed to find them.

The reason for traditional and predictable rituals became starkly obvious.

Betty, old windbag, piped up then, ahem-ing to clear her throat first. She sang as if to the river itself. And the river accepted the lament.

'Swing low sweet chariot, coming for to carry me home.'

The scene hushed to accommodate her voice. Ducks drifted on the current, the melody following slowly behind. Campers, including their dogs, stopped on the opposite bank to pay respect (or appreciate the spectacle). Their caravans hunkered down silently behind them. Windows shut their eyes. A single heron glided overhead; a semi-colon in the sky.

Tears prickled behind Maureen's eyes. As her remaining friend sang on, she remembered Lilith's laugh and her warmth and her small beaded handbag and her generosity with stories and her pregnant pauses and her perfect martinis and the huge gap she'd left in the world.

To bring herself back from the brink, Maureen made a quiet, cutting observation: 'So now the fat lady has sung.'

The daughter upended the urn as the last note rippled into the stratosphere.

Ashes dropped, gravity doing all the work with no breeze to take them. The daughter shook out the residue as you would pepper from a pepper shaker Lilith on her last casting.

The river rocks formed a quiet pool at the daughter's feet. Lilith became log-jammed there, a grey sludge on the water. She settled as the river rushed by.

30

The Tea Party

Zhang Ziyang

12th May 2017 – China 'spies on us and manipulates Chinese-language media' – *The Australian* – 'Outgoing Defence secretary Dennis Richardson has accused China of spying on Australia – Australia and China were not allies – "I think Australia's relationship with China and the US will continue to be able to be summarised simply: friends with both, allies with one" – "It is not secret that China is very active in intelligence activities directed against us" – "They do engage in some activities in their communities which I think would be considered unreasonable by most Australians"' – **12th May 2017 – Chinese spies 'very active' in Australia, departing defence secretary warns – ABC News** – 'His warnings follow similar concerns raised by former diplomat Chen Yonglin, who last year warned the number of Chinese spies and agents working in Australia was growing'...

* * *

Does it matter then, he asks himself, walking down Blackburn Road, towards Pinewood Shopping Centre. Does it matter that one must inevitably cease completely?[1] No, it doesn't – but when one is in one's twenties, it's too lovely a morning not to enjoy the sunshine, the baked cement roads and the eucalyptus greens. Yet, those noises of cars, s-car-s-car-s-car-s-car, pierce

---

1   "Did it matter then, she asked herself, walking towards Bond Street, did it matter that she must inevitably cease completely?" – Virginia Woolf, *Mrs. Dalloway.*

the harmony, and one is back to reality – the crossroads. 柳桉[2] waits there, till the traffic light flashing green bids him to go; but where? 'Mrs. Dalloway said she would buy the flowers herself.' Yes, 'I will buy the flowers myself,' he repeats, remembers, and moves on.

Once he arrives at Pinewood Asian Grocery, looking at buckets and buckets of flowers, what matters for him now is simply to pick, to choose, to be among them. He must buy a bunch himself. Chrysanthemums[3] perhaps, golden, earthy, plump, fit for the season of May, his mood of autumn; but oh, lilies, white-fragrant-flamboyant! Should he... Yet they never last, not for a week, a lifetime, the flower of death, only for a moment; but surely that is all that matters, the flower of rebirth – isn't it, between dying and living, dreams and reality, between China and Australia?

Between them, "to be, or not to be," he needs a ritual to decide – a party! – to be convinced, 'whether 'tis nobler in the mind to suffer,' or suppose he should leave... but to go back! That is a question too heavy for him now, too formless to ever give a thought. Laying lilies' head warmly on his elbow, one hand supporting firmly their bottom, ah, a baby in a cradle, he senses it all, the soft white petals, wide open, bursting a joy, a senseless joy in his chest. It simply couldn't happen in 'home', if China must be 'home', have flowers so easily, so impractical, so unrealistic, so... feminine. That word again! The meaning of it... a doll of China, one little boy, pale-fragile-delicate, cries in his chest. '爱哭鬼!—娘娘腔! !—男儿有泪不轻弹—[4]' the classmates, the teachers, oh, those people, and his mother comforting him, it would be easier for everybody if you don't cry in front of them, you know, your father never does... (只因未到伤心处[5]). The innocence of it, the naivety of lilies, one always understands so little about life.

He wishes to forget it, walking back to Normanby House, towards the accommodation for Monash students, just to dwell a little bit longer in the open air, slowly, slowly forgetting oneself, one's life under the sun. No, not even that is necessary... Sitting on the train, the raindrops spreading across the window, the scenery misty and blurry, millions and millions of droplets,

---

2   柳 – Willow (in Chinese, family name here); – Eucalyptus (in Chinese, given name here).

3   The flower of death in Chinese culture.

4   Crying Baby! – Sissy! – Men never easily weep – (in Chinese).

5   [Men never easily weep] / Till grief striking one's heart deep (in Chinese).

starting from the top, sinking, sin-king-sin-king-sin-king. The weight of the time, where would you go, where would we all go? – each of them, falling, twisting, struggling, till reaching there, the end of one's journey. He stared at his companion, a boy, lost, confused in the window, a pair of soft eyes, while rain was gliding over him. Alas, that was a rainy day in Australia. He sniffs the lilies and holds out one hand for the boy: 'to home? – To Home.'

12th May 2017—'Chinese are spying on us': veteran mandarin Dennis Richardson bows out – *The Guardian* **–** 'He said longevity hadn't conferred any special status, which made him somehow untouchable – "It wasn't different for me years ago. I have the advantage that I have a lot of Irish in my background and I like a fight – That is why the last four and a half years has been a laugh minute."'…

Home?! He doubts his answer and could almost laugh at it. Normanby House is only, after all, a temporary stay, and Australia, after four and a half years, one fails to grasp any sense of it. It is not exactly in-between, those British manners and American dreams. It is all at once, pleasure and pain, freedom and imprisonment, past and present, simply intertwined. One belongs here, but also somewhere else; one can become anybody, yet still remain nobody; one can be…

The Angel in the House. As soon as he arrives back at Normanby, ready to prepare the flowers, she slips behind him as he prepares the flowers and whispers: 'My dear, you are a young man. You are arranging a party that will be brilliant, amazing,[6] but you must have the help of a lady.' She blinks her eyes, and he can't resist but to hand her the scissors, the control, and one's existence. Dear, that is how you arrange it – she trims the leaves, measures the length, polishes the vase, pours the water, and fits them in. ~ Dôme épais le jasmin, À la rose s'assemble, Rive en fleurs, frais matin, Nous appellent ensemble ~[7] she hums it so ever softly, lest anyone suspect her presence; after

---

6 'She slipped behind me and whispered: "My dear, you are a young woman. You are writing about a book that has been written by a man…"' – Virginia Woolf, 'Professions for Women'.

7 From the Flower Duet in the opera *Lakmé* by Delibes: 'Thick dome of jasmine, Bends with the rose, Bank in bloom, fresh morning, Call us together'.

all, no one would understand, no one could share, she must be alone to be herself…

'A woman's whole life in a single day. Just one day. And in that day her whole life. It's one this day…'[8]

This day of all days, her fate becomes clear to her, she must decide. The party must be in the yard of Normanby, in an open space, on the wooden benches – blooming vigorous lilies surrounded by autumn maple leaves, crimson, delicate, falling. Ah, between these two rows of maple trees, it seems only yesterday, laying herself softly on one bench and holding a book, up, up! 'Oh, Mrs. Dalloway is always giving parties…' but the words escaped, only a blue pillowy sky, fresh green sprouts, and a sense of new-born left.

'One does not love a place the less for having suffered in it…'[9]

Alas, dwelling within the falling leaves, she yearns naturally for chrysanthemums, incurved petals embracing one heart, loveable and sorrowful, how could she 'forgo all the influence so sweet and so sad of the autumnal months'[10] for those unchangeable, uneventful and uncommunicative lilies? No, it is too late, everything done, no moment to be sentimental. She calms the boy's eyes – forget those, sweetie, they are not here anymore, only we are here, three of us – and asks him to jump, to run, to listen through cru-shing-cru-shing-cru-shing, the step against the fall: crisp; broken. She smiles at his innocent game – those sounds are nothing to him (perhaps nothing yet) – and lays the tablecloth ever so quietly, puts out the flourless orange cake, the vanilla lemon cheesecake, and a strawberry cream cake, pink, rosy, well, she feels that he may get away with it, and prepares a pot of Chinese black tea. She cannot think anything else, though as soon as she sits herself in the picture, the air becomes still, and the words can't help but just jump into her head: 'She is always giving parties to cover the silence.'[11]

'These were words which could not but dwell with her… They were of sobering tendency; they allayed agitation; they composed, and consequently must make her happier.'[12]

---

8   *The Hours* (film).

9   *Persuasion* (Jane Austen).

10   *Persuasion* (Jane Austen).

11   *The Hours* (Michael Cunningham).

12   *Persuasion* (Jane Austen).

Yet time must flow, guests must arrive, and it all starts now! If only dressed in a white muslin gown with delicate flowery embroideries, surrounded by them, she would seem to be a beaming lily full of love, simply to give, to share, to spread it even among the autumn leaves: 'Wouldn't you like to sit down? Wouldn't you like to have a cup of tea or a slice of cake? Wouldn't you...' smile, she would, in a simple smile, she would rejoice in all the compliments: 'Thanks for your invitation! – The cake is absolutely delicious! – What a brilliant idea to be here! – Lilies are stunning...' Yes, they are, they speak of beauty, though she knows they are not the sole speakers. The fallen leaves in a fragile voice, the autumn air in a melancholy tone, perhaps chrysanthemums and chrysanthemums alone can convey it all. There must be pleasures which can only arise from 'the tawny leaves and withered hedges, and from repeating to herself some few of the thousand poetical descriptions extant of autumn'[13] – '东篱把酒黄昏后, 有暗香盈袖. 莫道不消魂, 帘卷西风, 人比黄花瘦'[14] – Alas, there lilies must sing in a monotone, whilst here she stands, here she breathes, and here her eyes must sparkle to say: 'Thanks, my dear! – How lovely to have you here! – Isn't it wonderful? – Do, my darling, enjoy the lilies...' She is here, living, living in others, for others, in all those fictions, real feelings, real flesh.

But she isn't, isn't here, isn't anywhere in their eyes. Instead, he must be here. Yes, 柳桉 understands her pains, and here he dresses himself – black button-up shirt, dark indigo woollen vest, black leather belt, black cotton trousers, and black leather shoes – a gentleman in mourning. That is after all, the colour pattern for the party, black and white, life and death. Certainly, it is possible to die, to forget oneself, to be someone else. Indeed, a rebirth is in itself a form of death. But the arrival of another two guests draws him back, and surely, 'they would expect me to attend them myself,' thus he repeats, remembers (or does he forget) and moves towards them.

Mr. Blue with blue eyes, tall and slender, graceful and tasteful, who studies law and international relations, and Mr. Brown with brown hair, boyish and artless, sporty and earthy, who studies engineering and commence, yes,

---

13 *Persuasion* (Jane Austen).

14 'Besides the east hedge I drink after dusk; a subtle fragrance fills my sleeves. Don't say one is not pining away! When the west wind blows the blinds aside, I am frailer than the chrysanthemums' (Li QingZhao, Chinese female poet in Song Dynasty, translated by Jiaosheng Wang).

these are the gentlemen of order and reason, he thinks bitterly. Perhaps it is natural that he can't comprehend their interest in politics or history, for it has been through fiction that he has tasted the liberty, infinite readings, infinite meanings, infinite manners to be. Ah, to be like them, their ease with their manner, their speech, and simply being themselves, their confidence shines and blurs with the lilies, whilst he sits beside them as a quiet chrysanthemum, cuts their cake and pours their tea (he must have some strawberry cakes before all is gone). Yet to be with lilies, their youth stands out too much and for a moment suffocates him. Their beauty is everything he is not, and everything he is pains him. Infinite possibilities stir with him, the past, the present and perhaps the future – a second chance, a desire of rebirth, happiness and anticipation, yet denial, despair and death always follow a close step behind.

It was during a visit to the National Gallery of Victoria's Australia Section where the brilliance of the artistic expressions seized him – the exploration of early settlement, bewildering animals, gorgeous landscapes; the depiction of common life, the wool industry, husband and wife; the impression of movement and light, the shimmering fog, the flowing cloud… but romantic notion must exhaust in time. The war had changed everything. Pain and agony, twisting and stiffness, all firmly grasped him. Nonetheless, Mr. Blue and Mr. Brown seemed to disconnect themselves from the painting, as they were arguing about the Spanish Civil War. They were not feeling it, no, they couldn't, but dear, they must, for the two of them knew so much injustice within each government towards their people. Oh, those people, indigenous ones, immigrant ones, lower class, working class, and they were to attend the protest later to support refugee people, how silly of him to invite them here, to merely admire! Yes, they must, *must*... Indeed, what of him, with his clichéd feelings, clichéd ways of looking – those dead long faces on the wall staring at him; his smile frozen, fixed, becoming permanent – one should have been happy, been grateful to be here…

Really, here again with them, quietly drinking his tea (he is too late, the cake all gone), she shouldn't have given them all, but he knows she couldn't help it, and he couldn't help joining them, though he does wish to enter their conversation, he has already learnt to stop making any meaning of it, from past to present, their dialogue almost exists in his mind as a single unity:

'–the Black War in Tasmania is totally an act of genocide – more than eight hundred aboriginals against around two hundred colonists – death rate, four against one – the remained aboriginals were first moved to Flinders Island – just another cultural genocide—European diseases—Dr Henry Jeanneret versus Robert Clark – the petition was unreliable – mind you, aboriginals were never the power player –

– eight hundred and fifty asylum seekers on Manus Island – poor hygiene – the Papua New Guinean Supreme Court ruled it illegal – official refugees now – not welcomed by the Australian government – apartheid – South Africa – racial segregation – America – plantations in the South – the distribution of wealth is unfair – can you believe that Donald Trump – true, she was not the best option, but – so glad that Macron has won the election – after Trump – Le Pen around 34 percent–' (and they continue about the future of La France, they continue, continue…)

He still remembers, on the same day after the protest, two of them were debating intensely about dictatorship near Federation Square, whereas he could only cast his eyes on a nearby lawn, watching the sparrows, oh, those grey-brown little fellows, jumping, playing, chirping – children running in a playground. It has become another picture in his heart, to create this sense of artistic serenity. Ah, art has no nationality, the artist has no nationality, and here he is, to be bounded by no obligation to be an Australian, forever free, forever imprisoned not to be.

'All this must go on without me; should I resent it, or…'[15]

Here comes Miss Dolly (how glad he can quit them now, how burdensome that he must join her now), with her doll-like eyes behind an old-fashioned pair of glasses, independent and approachable, active and talkative, and wasn't she in a 旗袍[16], embroidered in rosy pink plump blossoms, attending the MRS[17] Ball? It is as well that she studies education, for she reminds the boy too much of his own Chinese teachers and terrifies him a little. Yes, in front of her, 柳桉 can't make any complaint about China, its air pollution, its educational system, its restraint, and equally any praise on

---

15 'All this must go on without her; did she resent it, or…' – Virginia Woolf, *Mrs. Dalloway*.
16 Cheongsam (in Chinese).
17 Monash Residential Services.

Australia is deemed as a betrayal (except perhaps on women's right). She truly rejoices in her freedom, whereas he must be contented with: 'It's a pleasure to have you here! How was your placement, your students, your working?' All must be shadowed by the boy's fear, yet he knows she means no harm at all. Though still once the boy trembled at her voice: 'How could you call yourself Chinese if you don't know how to make dumplings?' Yes, she meant no harm, the lady could only smile, and tried her best to help her prepare her weekly menu, wrapping the dumplings very clumsily, and Miss Dolly was all gratitude. As for 柳桉, he also laughed once at her reason for not studying in China: '不是中国教育的问题，是我自身不适应而已。'[18] There she made excuses, and here she argued, but she is always in confidence: 'Ha, the placement has finished weeks ago, don't you remember – I've told you that they were quite cute – Well, the work is still very busy – It is wonderful to have the Chinese tea here – I've missed the taste so much – Well, the work is still very busy –'.

Perhaps it is his own fault that he only masters the art of obedience and silence, his inability to convey it all, to articulate his feelings, and he can only sigh in his heart each time a single leaf falls down ever so quietly on the wooden benches. As soon as he sits himself softly there in the party, the time seems to become still, and the laughter and the joy are just filling the crack of each heart, at least he feels it to be so, and knows what to expect: 'Oh, such a lovely party! – It is an absolute delight! – Thanks so much for it!' Is that all? That all he does, to bring them together, flowers and guests, beauty and delight, is that all that matters? He must smile (why must?) at their happiness, dancing plates, spinning cups, flowing words in-between, laughing eyebrows, swinging figures, floating senses to connect. As a whole, a unity, they seem to imprint it all in this moment, a picture of eternity, a picture of full pleasure. But he isn't there, he isn't anywhere in this picture. He is just a beholder, merely to immortalise a moment in others' lives as self-indulgence, as if the purpose of it is to wait for the still butterfly to fly again, and to bring oneself a sense of being. Yet it is inevitable that the party must be over, one must cease to be, and what's left becomes almost a self-punishment, spoiling one's life not to be oneself. Surely it doesn't matter whether he exists or not.

---

18 'It is not the fault of Chinese education, it is merely myself who can't fit in' (in Chinese).

Life continues, time moves on, and pictures stay, while right now, the lilies are blooming so...

...ever so brightly. Yes, there in the vase, the chrysanthemums are echoing an autumn symphony. I listen in bliss, and the chorus of golden leaves in a golden weather shines ever so brightly. 'Oh, dear Alice, wouldn't you have another cup?' I taste rosy pink and welcome our new guest whilst the lady, Miss Hare, cuts Alice a slice of cake; she can't help but put a single chrysanthemum behind Alice's ear, 'It suits you, sweetie.' In the meantime, the boy – little Mouse, energetic, lively, can't hide his excitement – runs across the tea table to meet her, 'Alice, Alice, let's play, let's play!' How sweet, how lovely, I turn aside and find Miss Mantis in her brown gown[19] nods approvingly at Alice, for she has let the little Mouse dance on her hand, whilst Mr. Cicada in his green suit[20] is playing a country tune on his fiddle. It makes me even happier to see Miss Spider knitting pairs of gloves, she looks so pretty in her black dress with a red ribbon tied behind her back, while Mr. Swan is so kind to read poems to her in his black suit. Ah, I adjust my top hat (pink!), how wonderful to be here, and take a sip of tea slowly and eat one rosy cake after another. Yes, to dwell here just a little bit longer, a bit longer...

Until it all must end, inevitably, he knows it will be so, must be so (the party over) – **21st May 2017 – Australia first: what new visa policy means for Chinese, Asian immigrants – South China Morning Post** – 'In a budget unveiled last week, the Australian government of Malcolm Turnbull put "Australians first" by cutting the 457 visa for foreign workers and bringing in tougher English testing for immigrants –'

Yes, to stand still, to cease completely, we hear the leaves falling, then the cru-shing-cru-shing...

---

19 *Archimantis latisyla*, a species of mantid native to Australia, has a brown body.
20 *Cyclochila australasiae*, a species of cicada and commonly found in Australia, has a green body.

31

Obsession

Callum Methven

'... My ex-wife... she thought she was going crazy.'

She wasn't.

'... You know: hearing voices and all that...'

She was.

He buried his hands further into the pockets of his tattered hoodie; his eyes never left the floor. 'I've gotta admit, I thought the doc was full of shit. I didn't think it... I mean, I don't think anybody did – not even her – not really. But then we saw the news reports that night. And the next night, and the next after that, and they all started saying the same thing. The government on high alert... Mind readers all over the world... What a joke.'

I was drifting in and out of the room. I was trying to line my chair up with those of the two people either side of me, but I couldn't get it right; the invisible lines that were as real as ever kept crossing over one another and so I had to tap my feet on the floor six times just to make it right.

No one had seemed to notice just yet, but I knew that they were only being polite. They could only ignore the sound of chair legs scraping across the wooden floor for so long before they would start staring at me. Sometimes I wished I could read minds, just so I would know whether people were thinking about me or not. The thought made me squirm even more.

* * *

I didn't know anybody who had been directly affected by the Revelation; at least not intimately. A girl that I used to go to school with was outed online.

Another man, one of the clinicians at the hospital where I worked, quit his job the very day he realised, left to make the most of his situation and try his hand at selling his new talents. I didn't even take much notice of the news until I crossed a group of people on the street wearing tinfoil hats.

I buried my hands in my pockets that day, not taking my eyes off of the ground lest I make a wrong step and have to retake it in public. The tighter I kept my gloved fists clenched the easier it became, for a single moment, to plug the crack where the thoughts leaked into my brain. Oncoming traffic in my own inner voice.

The psychiatrists' clinic was a small room on the fourth floor of an old office building. The lift always creaked on the way up. I blinked six times when I reached my floor, stepping out on my left foot when the doors opened. I smiled tight-lipped to the receptionist and took a seat in closest the window.

It was ten minutes past twelve when the door to Dr Kim's office opened.

'Oh... Lucy's here, Kim,' said the receptionist, suddenly alert.

'I can see that,' said the Doctor. 'Lucy, why don't you come in?'

* * *

It seemed an even tighter space when the door clicked shut behind me. Three of the four walls were layered from top to tail with heavy tomes with titles such as *How to talk about Depression* and *DSM-6: American Psychiatric Association*. There was a tall man sitting in the corner wearing a lab coat, a notepad and pen in his hands. He had never been there in any of my previous sessions. He did not take his eyes off of me. We sat down.

'Oh, don't worry about him,' said Kim, when she saw my face. 'This is Tim. Tim is going to sit in on your appointment today and take some notes. Is that okay?'

I straightened my chair just as another violent image projected across the theatre of my mind. 'Um... sure, I guess,' I said.

'Fantastic.' Kim loaded up a fresh document on her computer. 'Now, Lucy: the last time I saw you was...'

Three weeks ago.

'... That's right. And how have you been since – mood-wise?'

'I, um...' My eyes darted from my doctor to the man in the corner, his pen hovering above the paper as if waiting for me to speak. I told her I was alright, at least until I was rostered on for four nights in a row. 'I know, I know what you said about shift-work, but... I need the money. I know what you said about the hospital too, but it's not like I'm qualified to work anywhere else...'

Tim was scribbling quietly, his legs crossed and his shoulders hunched over, his hand sweeping across the page back and forth as he wrote.

'So the compulsions have gotten worse... Would you say, much worse, or just moderately worse?' said Kim.

Moderately worse, I replied. *I think.*

'What's been the worst these past weeks?'

A shrug.

'Which takes the most time out of your day?'

The counting, I told her. I see everything in sixes.

Kim was typing rapidly. 'What do you mean by 'everything'?' she said.

She couldn't feel them, the lines. There are lines everywhere, I told her, invisible lines between points on the ground where I have to walk, same as before, and my brain puts everything into categories and I count the parts of the categories, I count the beats in a song, I count my steps down the stairs, and if I don't finish on a multiple of six, I...

'What happens?'

It doesn't go very well.

Kim finished transcribing the sentence and tapped the Enter button several times. She shifted her gaze back to me, occasionally sparing a glance for the mystery scribe in the corner.

'You're on one hundred milligrams of Anafranil at the moment, of course,' said Kim. 'And...'

'Twenty mil of Lexapro,' I said.

'That's right.'

Please don't make me take more Lexapro.

I held my hands in my lap, twitching my fingers so that they might feel even against one another. It did not work. I eyed the man in the corner with a certain distrust and he watched me back as if I were an interesting experiment.

When my psychiatrist met my gaze the next time I knew what was coming.

'Lucy,' said Kim, 'how are you going with regards to the obsessions? Have you had to deal with many of your... dark thoughts... lately?'

For a moment I considered asking for my prescriptions and walking out the door. I didn't talk about the thoughts to anyone. These were not things that you could say out loud. And still the man in the corner was waiting for my next word.

'I... it's been okay, recently,' I said eventually. 'But they're always there. It's like... it's like there's someone else in my head, using my own thinking voice, trying to make me...'

Trying to make me want to kill myself, I thought.

'This is perfectly normal for someone with your condition,' said Kim. 'And these thoughts that aren't your own, do they tend be violent, or –?'

'Violent... and sexually inappropriate...' I said. '...It depends on the situation, but... well, both. It's always there. Like when I'm stopping at a red light, or when my sister Lauren brings the kids over, or... or when I'm cutting vegetables and I have the knife in my hand. Sometimes I can ignore it and sometimes I can't. I know it makes my... my habits... even worse, though. I guess it's a good thing there's so much white noise in my head... The noise drives me crazy, but at least I know I'm still me. With this... I don't know anything anymore...'

* * *

The doors were nearly closed when somebody called out. I placed my hand on the closing doors and they stayed open.

'Thank you,' said the man called Tim, pushing his askew glasses further up his nose. He held a briefcase in his left hand. 'I didn't think I was going to make it.'

I said nothing.

My left hand touched my side but I dared not make it even in such a closed space.

The doors slid shut and we began to descend. The man called Tim placed his other hand in his white lab coat. I saw him steal a glance at me in the mirror but when I looked back he seemed focussed on one of the buttons of his lab coat.

'Are you a mind-reader?' I blurted.

'Sorry?' said the man called Tim. 'Ah, no, no.' He readjusted his glasses again with a single finger. '... I'm actually here on behalf of the government.'

'The government?'

'Yes, it's rather a long story.'

The lift stopped at the ground floor. I was ready to make a bee-line for the building entrance, but instead I turned on the spot.

'Why were you in my appointment today?' I said.

'I came here today with a proposal for you,' said Tim. 'Do you have a moment?'

'I... I guess so.' I walked alongside him through the empty lobby and we crossed the threshold to the frigid outside world. 'I, um... What kind of proposal is this exactly?'

'A job opportunity.'

'What kind of job opportunity?'

A black four-wheel drive pulled around the corner, slamming to a stop before us. I considered dashing back into the building and slamming the door behind me but I froze.

'Why don't you come with me and we'll talk about it on the way?' said Tim.

'Do I have a choice?' I said.

'Of course, Lucy. You always have a choice.'

* * *

I don't know what possessed me to go with him. But he was one of those people – not a mind-reader, no – he was trusting.

Beyond the film of the blackened window the city of Wellington drifted past uneasily. He asked me all kinds of questions. What do you know about the Revelation? How would you describe your illness? How long have you had symptoms?

After following a long path downhill, the car lurched to the left and I could see the water of the bay. We navigated a series of industrial hubs that extended onto the most-recently reclaimed stretch of waterfront. Then we turned to an underground carpark. I asked him where we were going, but he wouldn't say.

The car came to a stop between the lines in an empty lot. Tim stepped out of the vehicle and I did likewise.

Tim walked towards a singular lift, with me by his side, and the driver with my bag trotted along behind us, three sets of uneven footsteps echoing in the still. The carpark itself was a polished, empty plain, the only light flickering from evenly-spaced fluorescent tubes trapped likewise beneath forty floors of just-as-empty office blocks.

I swallowed as we began to sink downward, down beneath the ground. 'Where are we going, exactly?' I said.

'That's a good question. We'll be working on behalf of the Defence Department,' said Tim, as if that answered my question.

With a gentle chime the doors to the lift slid open once more, revealing a sterile white reception with nobody behind the desk and not even a draught between the furthest wall and the end of the corridor.

Tim beckoned me to follow him. My hands were beginning to sweat but I did as I was told. We walked along the passageway before coming to a stop before a door to their left. The silent driver handed me back my bag and Tim held the door open. I entered a small office space, not unlike that of Doctor Kim, but rather than my psychiatrist a woman in a dark suit sat across the desk.

'Please, take a seat,' said Tim.

I did so. I held my bag in my lap. The woman in the suit did not shift her dark gaze an inch.

'Ms Simms,' said Tim, 'I'd like you to meet Worthgate. She is the head of the Agency's Intelligence department. She will be in charge of this project, at least from a legal standpoint; myself and my team will be taking care of the analysis aspect.'

I felt my insides squirm. 'Please tell me why I'm here,' I said.

The woman known as Worthgate let the edge of a smile into the corners of her mouth. 'We've been exposed, and the ship is sinking,' she said. 'You're here to plug the holes.'

* * *

There is a certain way of doing things, at least in my head. You have to do it until it feels right. Like when I turned the tap on. *One, two, three, four, five, six.* I ran my hands under the cold water, wrapped my hands together and rubbed them from left to right and top to bottom. *One, two, three, four, five, six. One, two, three, four, five, six.* I turned the tap off. I flicked the water from my hands. I clapped my hands together and buried them in the hand towel. *One-two-three-four-five-six-one-two-three-four-five-six-six-six-six-six-six-s-s-s...*

'God*dammit,*' I muttered to my own reflection.

The woman in the mirror was worn out, even though I had been all but locked up in the same hotel room for a week with a double bed and personal room service.

It took three more tries to get it right, washing my hands.

Then I threw myself down on the bed and tried not to move. Until there came a knock on the door.

It was Tim, accompanied by Lenny, the young graduate student who had introduced herself to me upon my arrival at the hotel exactly seven days ago.

'Good morning, Ms Simms,' said Tim.

'Hi Lucy,' said Lenny. 'How are you?'

'Are you ready for the big day?'

I wiped my eyes; both of them at the same time. I knew that I needed to redo it – it was crooked, and I could still feel the uneven pressure of the back of my knuckles on my eyes – but the pair were watching me and waiting for me and I knew that there would be no way for me to hide it.

* * *

The plain navy carpet that canvassed the floors of every room in the underground facility would have come as a welcome relief if it weren't for all of the closed doors drawing their lines in unwelcome directions, making the walk back to the lift ever more difficult to navigate.

I sighed when the doors slid shut; I blinked down six times.

'We're going to sit you in one of our interview rooms,' said Tim, 'and bring in each of the... employees... one at a time, so that you can have a chat with them. The hope is that they'll feel comfortable enough to confess their reading ability – well, if indeed the individual is capable of such things.'

'You just want me to talk to them?' I said. I took two small steps so that my last right step on the blue in the carpet was my sixth. The relief lasted about until I put my left foot down in the black square.

Tim smiled. 'Pretty much.'

'Pretty much?'

'I mean, yes,' and he gave an uncomfortable chuckle.

* * *

I cast my gaze down upon the wooden table and blinked my eyes shut; blinked hard six more times without really opening them. I focussed on the perfect symmetry of the door handle, the way its slight shadow seemed to be its pair.

Then the door handle moved downwards.

A young man in a suit entered, his spikey hair gelled back and a lanyard lay around his neck that I couldn't quite make out. His eyes never sat still, darting from me to the glass and to the cameras that he must have known were watching in every corner.

'At your leisure,' I heard Tim's voice over the intercom.

The young man in the suit sat down in the seat across from me.

'Um... Hello,' I said, never less sure of myself. 'I... I'm Lucy... I'm not entirely sure how this works.'

For a long moment he simply stared at me without saying anything. He stared at me; looked me in the eye and didn't look away, even when I clearly became uncomfortable.

Then his face cringed inward. He shook his head.

'What are you doing to me?' he mumbled.

My throat ran dry. 'W-what?'

'Make... make it stop! MAKE IT STOP!'

He shook his head from side to side like he was trying to shake it loose from his neck.

Then he smashed himself against the table.

ONE-TWO-THREE-FOUR-FIVE-SIX.

* * *

Most of them bled, I told her as I gathered my coat. You'd be amazed how much a person can bleed from their nose... I wiped my own nose each side; three with one hand and three with the other, then the reverse.

The colours were coming back to me then, the crisp greys, the fluorescent light. I tried to focus on Mary-Anne, or at least her silhouette, the blue gems that sparkled in her ears even inside from the overcast.

'And your medication hasn't worked since?' she said. She opened the door for me and a cold draught swept through. 'That's horrible.'

I shrugged again, told her I could live with it.

'But you shouldn't have to!'

She offered me a lift, kind woman, but I told her that I was waiting for someone. 'Go on without me,' I said, 'I'll see you next week.'

* * *

As if like clockwork, the black four-wheel drive pulled up just as the rain began to pour. The window rolled down.

'You know, you're not supposed to talk about it,' said Tim.

He opened the door and moved across so that I could have a seat. I tucked my bag under my arm and closed the door. The car began moving.

'I know,' I said, 'but –'

'Better to talk to strangers than your own family, yes.'

My knees were rubbing together in my jeans but I couldn't make them line up. I asked him where we were going.

'The airport,' said Tim, 'same as last time.'

'And how much will I be paid?'

He shrugged. 'The same as last time, Lucy Simms.'

We stopped at a red light and the rain drummed against the soulless windscreen.

One-two-three-four-five-six.

One-two-three-four-five-six.

One-two-three-four-five-six.

32

A Good/Strange Thing

Leah De Forest

In fifteen minutes Alessa is going to die. Because of this her age is relevant. We measure our longevity against hers, weigh the level of tragedy. So young, but – her children no longer babies. So young, but – three years past forty.

Alessa is in a queue. The line is thick and hot with bodies; the sun merciless; the air full of loudspeaker cheer. *Comeonladies-andgentlemen-areyou-ready-toride!!* And whoosh-doof-doof. Alessa's bag contains a full day's worth of snacks (pretzel sticks, raisins, cereal bars), a water bottle for each child and her husband's Xanax. She has decided that they will have a good day: sweaty-smiling selfies for the holiday card, family in-jokes, a respite from the sense that the world out there is doomed, that they (as in they, them, us) have ruined everything.

'Hey, Mom.' This is Sophie, Alessa's eldest. She's just hit her growth spurt, all elbows and limbs, her nose too long for her face. 'Check out that woman, right? She just ate like five donuts. While standing in *line*.'

'Okay, Soph.' Alessa digs around in her bag. 'Are you telling me you're hungry? I have your pretzel sticks –'

'Ugh, *no*.' Sophie hugs her stomach. 'I couldn't possibly eat after seeing *that*.'

'Listen, Sophie. I don't think –' she looks around at the throng of baseball caps and tank tops, armpit hair, bellies. Her daughter's fine, fair hair. 'Just keep your voice down, all right?'

Alessa's smile touches only one cheek. The sun is warm, at least. Mark's hand pleasantly heavy on her shoulder, and Eve's swinging feet only mildly irritating. Thud. Thigh. Thwack. Eve is six and too big to be hanging off Mark's hip. But Eve understands the need for it, the way her weight helps her father stand and breathe and see. Zac keeps himself off to the left, grinding the toe of his Converse into the crumbling pavement. He is unable to give even one tiny shit about how uneasy his father is. Alessa has tried explaining, neurochemistry and flight or fight, childhood trauma, that too, really, but Zac turns away or wrinkles his ten-year-old nose. He is a kind boy who loves his sisters, but he cannot stand weakness.

'So!' Alessa claps so enthusiastically that the short man to their right grabs his hat. 'Favourite thing so far?'

'Breakfast,' Zac says, flicking imaginary crumbs off his *Leader of the Pack* (wolf) T-shirt.

'Are you kidding me?' says Sophie. 'Motel pancakes? I –'

'Spending time with everyone!' Eve slings her arm forward to grab Alessa's neck, almost knocking her parents' heads together in the process. Her breath smells of apples. 'Family us!'

'Yeah.' Mark tilts his forehead towards Alessa's. Sweat sticks between their skin. He forgot his hat and won't wear sunscreen; he worries about cancer and is paralysed between his fear of the sun and of chemicals. Tonight, Alessa thinks, his speckled nose and arms and balding head will be dark pink and hot, and he'll try so hard to keep his I'm-dying thoughts inside. Alessa shuffles closer so she can reach an arm around both Eve and Mark. Feel the warm lumps of their bodies. The detergent-sweet-funk of them.

'I think I liked the Pirate Ship best.' Alessa smiles into the sun. The clouds are postcard fluff dots. 'But RumbleRapids looks awesome too. And it's still early.'

'Yeah.' Zac snips a look at her. 'I'm so glad we drove five hours north for this.'

'Hm.' This is Alessa's cheerfully-ignoring-you noise. Zac pushes his moppish hair back off his face and goes back to staring at the ground. The truth is, the Pirate Ship makes Alessa feel like her stomach is being filled with somebody else's vomit. But she doesn't want to give Mark any more reasons. That is to say, she wants him to focus on the fun part, all the ways in which he's going to be fine. He'd stayed in the Pirate Ship line right up until the last second, cheerfully certain that yes, he would use his ticket. But then he had a problem with his shoe, the kind that involved hot cheeks and pale, shaking hands. He wanted to ride, he wanted to be okay. He just wasn't. So the others went right ahead, as Mark suggested, and they waved like happy maniacs each time the garish vessel swung past him. Squeezed in the hot plastic seat between Zac and Eve, Alessa watched the simulated danger on her children's faces, gripped the metal lap bar, and grinned her way through the bile swirling up her throat. All of this was pretty much awful, but there was one good/strange thing. When the ship had swung back almost to its peak, nearly vertical, gravity tugging at them, Alessa glanced to the left and saw not her husband or the amusement park but a wide clear field. She blinked. Now a crater, blackened destruction, the scorched future she read about every day in the news but couldn't quite enter. Then the down swing. Stomach acid pushed up to the base of her tongue, her children screamed, varying degrees of delight and fear. On the next upswing she tried to see it again, but the regular world was back. Blue sky and green leaves and people walking by. She got off the ride nauseated and diffusely disappointed.

Alessa and her family are now about twenty people from the front of the RumbleRapids line. It's like being in rush hour traffic, without the facial expressions and gesticulations: everyone's elbows tucked and exasperation aimed carefully at the sky. The young guy taking tickets has sweated a wide line down the back of his red DreamPark T-shirt. As each group shuffles up, he recites variations of 'how you doing?' and 'hey, how's it going?', the intonation ping-ponging as his slender fingers take the pink perforated tickets, tear them, and hand back the stubs. 'Souvenir,' he says to one little kid, who adjusts her Dora the Explorer sun hat and looks the other way. 'Or not,' he chuckles, watching the raft that just got loaded ascend the first watery hill. He stares for a long time, ignoring the next group of Hawaiian shirted young men, perhaps on some corporate bonding retreat, who clearly want to ask him a question. Alessa cheers him. Go you, young man. Feel free. Think your thoughts. Don't be –

'Mom?' Eve wriggles down her father's leg and grabs Alessa's elbow. 'I need to pee.' The last word a hot whisper.

Of course, now that they're just a few people away from the head of the queue. Eve's holding the front of her shorts and looking mortified and Mark is suddenly staring the other way. Red goose pimples up the side of his neck, finger and thumb working at the hem of his pastel yellow shirt.

'Okay, sweetie.' Alessa smiles. 'The bathroom's just this way.'

She grips Eve's sweaty meaty fingers a little too tight, hauls her out through the crowd. Eve has to skip unevenly to keep up. Alessa can't see her, she's focused forward on the throng of heads and shoulders and overlarge backpacks, but she knows how it is: small bit lip, thin brown hair stuck to her forehead, soft pouch of belly above her jean shorts. Every precious painful irritation. A stream of praise and condemnation runs through Alessa's brain like background code. Sweet smile jagged teeth trusting nature gullible eats too much. Up too early steals things panders to her father. Full of soft promise and easy love.

There is a line ten people deep outside the women's room. Eve says nothing but emits a small whimper. 'Mom,' she hisses. 'I really gotta *go*.' She shuffles from one foot to the other. The tall woman in front turns and offers a sym-pathetic smile. Alessa squeezes Eve's hand.

'It won't be long, sweetie.'

They both know this is a lie. That the woman in front will not relinquish her place in the line (somehow her turquoise blouse and wide-brimmed hat telegraph this fact). They also know that Eve's bladder has never been strong; that she drank three glasses of juice at breakfast; and that every other person in this line has probably already consumed at least one huge slushie, or at the very least an ice cream, and they all have to allow time to undo their clothing, squat over the warm, wet toilet seats, wipe and flush, and that there is no quick bathroom solution if you were born with girl parts.

Eve has been saving her favourite shorts for this special day, and she loves them because they have a tiny sparkling unicorn on the rolled-up hem.

Eve makes a low, uh-oh-now sound.

'Okay, sweetie.'

But a line is a line, and pushing through would require either meekness or assertiveness, neither of which Alessa has in reserve right now. She feels a soft pop, a sensation of blooming – irritation? Rage? – in her shoulder. Alessa adjusts her posture, places her hand briefly on the back of Eve's head. *Everythinghappyfine*. Eyes ahead. The turquoise woman is standing very close and she smells of oats. Sweat gathers along the woman's neck crease, a shining line that runs from behind her ear to the front of her neck. Above that line an earring hangs: small, ceramic, white. It shivers with the woman's every movement, the tiny weight of the ceramic exaggerated by the pivot of the fine gold hoop that attaches to her lobe. Alessa squints. What is it – four legs? Mouse, hamster, horse? She leans, almost touching. The woman must surely feel breath on the back of her neck, but she doesn't turn. Only shakes her head a little. The earring figure swivels and there it is, a tiny ceramic dog, clumsy factory-drawn brindle markings down its back. A second good/strange thing yawns in Alessa's mind: the black crater/green field, flickering back and forth, fast as an old film. The dog runs across both scenes in quick, long leaps. Maybe the tiny thing has teeth. For gnawing tiny bones, stripping flesh and sucking out marrow. Or maybe it eats soft food from a can, naps and yelps softly in its dreams.

The unknowing is both torture and joy.

Alessa drops her hand behind her, extending her fingers for Eve's grasp.

'Eve?'

Jesus.

'Eve?'

Shit. Shit. Heart beat-beat-beat and the thought: *it would be my fault.*

Alessa pushes past the turquoise woman, neck craned, elbows out. All these people, not one of them the right one. Alessa goes into the bathroom, puffs her cheeks against the smell of piss and bleach. Slaps each metal cubicle door. She keeps her voice inquisitive with an upward tick.

'Eve? You there?'

Maybe Eve went to the RumbleRapids line. Or she's waiting out by the ice creams.

Back outside, the light near blinds and the turquoise woman is standing near the head of the line, reading something on an ancient, shiny Blackberry. Alessa pans her face across the blurring scene.

'Mom!'

'Jesus! Eve!'

The child is squatting between two low bushes behind the bathroom block, a huge grin on her face. 'I peed!' she calls. 'And not in my unicorn shorts!' She fist pumps so hard she almost topples back into the garden bed and Alessa drops her head back, lets out a jagged laugh. Relief almost brings her undone at the knees. She leads Eve into the bathroom so she can wash her hands with cold water and the last drop of soap.

* * *

'Oh, hey!' Mark's arm sways high above the other heads in the RumbleRapids line. 'Over here!'

Eve grips Alessa's hand and pulls in front, dragging Alessa through the crowd. 'The line was so long!' Eve says, leaning up onto tip-toes as soon as they get close. 'I had to imprompovise, I went –'

'Oh? Great!' Mark runs his hand over his sweaty scalp. His cheeks are petri-dish flushed. 'Listen, hey, we've been at the start of the line for a little while, and the guy says – now that you're here it's our turn! We're on the next raft. How does that sound?'

Sweat has soaked halfway down the sides of Mark's shirt. One hand grips the chipped-paint rail that leads to the steps.

'I think,' Zac breezes past, hands the attendant his ticket. 'We should just get on with it.'

Alessa stands behind Mark, fixes her face with a smile.

Sophie passes in her ticket. 'You know what, Dad,' she says, glancing at the attendant, looking back at her mother. A quick glance through her eyelashes. 'It sounds like Eve didn't finish telling you what happened. Maybe you guys could –'

Mark takes an immediate step backwards, clodding into Alessa. His voice slaps like a palm on water. 'You want an ice cream, Eve? Does that sound good?'

Alessa rubs her mildly mashed foot against her right calf. She puts a hand on her daughter's small shoulder, drops her voice to pleased. 'You could show Dad where the ice cream cart is.'

The attendant coughs abruptly and a man behind them lets out a hot sigh.

'Yeah.' Eve palms the hair off her forehead and looks back up at her mother. 'We could go on the water ride after. When there's less people.' From above, her smile is mostly bottom teeth.

'Great!' Alessa digs in her bag for her ticket and brushes Mark's cheek with a kiss.

'Thank you,' he whispers, placing three fingers on her upper arm. A lifetime, there, of love and pain and negotiation.

'Of course,' Alessa says. A brief moment of eye contact and he slips from the crowd.

'Allllll right!' the attendant sings, reaching behind Alessa to replace the chain barrier. He clicks it with the force of a spider-smash. 'If you'll just take your places on that side of the raft, wonderful! Don't forget your lap belts!'

Alessa seats herself between Sophie and Zac, bringing the thick Velcro strap around her middle and sticking it firmly over her belly. She glances at Zac, who places a hand over his half-heartedly attached belt and calls out to Eve. 'Hey! Woohoo!' His voice is genuinely upbeat. He gives a long arc of a wave.

The raft is round and dark green, smaller than it looked from the line. They sit at twelve, four, and eight o'clock, their knees almost touching in the centre. The water underneath begins to churn and an attendant scoots past to tap each of their belts. She wears a DreamPark cap backwards, her red T-shirt knotted above her tight belly. On the young woman's hand signal, the raft begins to climb the first mechanised hill. The wind picks up a fine chlorinated spray and the soft sides of the raft press into Alessa's aching back. She smiles and taps Sophie on the knee, next to the small constellation of freckles. Sophie nods and cranes her neck away, taking in the emerging view. Sun and trees and colour and fun. Alessa flattens the hem of her taupe shorts against her thighs, watches the small disc of water in the bottom of the raft flatten and finger and spin. The ride reaches the top of the first hill, pivots and descends in a short rush. Alessa closes her eyes and lets her insides knock around, listens to the small happy sounds her children make as the raft climbs and spins and drops and turns, spraying and sliding, taking them –

The raft shudders, slows.

Alessa opens her eyes wide but it happens so fast. The raft tips. The world turns. She sees flashes: Zac's wide-open mouth. A wedge of sparkling water. Sophie's palm. The planet slows and it feels as if her spine is flying out of her body. Pain twists and cracks. The tip-over completes and then she's underneath and it's dark and her legs sting and her brain tries to see –

It shows her a wide frozen river, glossy with semi-melt

And right out deep in the middle. The brindle dog.

Real now.

Large.

With fur and teeth and claws.

It stands in a puddle which is perhaps six feet in circumference, its face arranged into something like hope although it's obviously stuck.

Alessa tries to take a breath.

But only her dream-mouth answers.

This is.

Not

The dog is calm. Standing there. The pink pads of its feet must be cold but it doesn't shift its weight. Wind whips up at its face. Smell of pine needles and gasoline.

Alessa is alone. My children, my children, where –

Ripped away

The dog wants nothing. Raft water from RumbleRapids crosses into the frozen river, blurring the dog's face, smattering its back; it does not respond. Alessa watches those drops, stares at them hard. Trying to hold on, to hold in, swallow and own her last glimpse of the world. Then the raft water is gone and the dog splays its legs, all four, all at once, impossible, its ribcage sliding into that shallow puddle and its head turning, side-on now, a triangular terror-smile, a child's teeth inside.

The dog boats its legs along the ice, still splayed, like a water bug trying but

Still

Like

The way a dog's ribcage is pointed, a whorl of hair at the peak, pointing down at the earth the dog passes over when it walks explores eats shits pisses grins

Muscles bone flesh cracks

Water

Chlorine

Maybe the dog will stay until the looming terrors come, and when it all ends the dog will break into a run, because –

33

Strings

Vanessa Proctor

A triple strand of natural pearls…
pink, symmetrical, radiant
with orient lustre – it was nearly
divided into single ropes
by three sisters going over
the spoils of their mother's will.
More pearls among pearls
looped over diamond rings
and gemstone brooches.

But by some small miracle
they changed their minds,
decided to give it to your father
who had been left nothing,
so that you could have it.
So it could hang around
your lovely neck.
So your lifeblood could
warm it, make it shine.

Tears of the gods now tie you
to women whose hearts,
once open, lost their lustre
and slowly hardened
into deep sea pearls.

34

All That Is Offered

Magdalena McGuire

We sat together in the assembly area, Zena's bare knees touching mine. Around us, people giggled and shoved. I moved closer to my friend and breathed in her coconut-hair. She smelt of afternoons by the pool, of teen-agers oiling themselves in the sun. She was a holiday from the BO that leaked from the pores of the school.

'It pongs out here,' I said.

'Yeah,' Zena said. 'It's gross.' She clasped her hands around her throat and gagged. Our heads bent together; we laughed. I wiped my eyes and swallowed hard as our principal, Mrs Gogniat, marched to the front of the assembly area, a microphone in one hand. Today she wore beige shorts, knee-length, like a tourist.

All the real tourists had fled because it was the Build-Up now, the sticky bridge between seasons. We could forget about it in our air-conditioned classroom with the picture of the Swiss Alps pinned by the door. But not out here. The assembly area, with its concrete floor and aluminium roof, offered no protection from the heat. There were no walls and I could see out to the oval where a group of ibises picked their way across the grass. Instead of a song they offered an ugly croak. *Ark, ark, ark.*

Mrs Gogniat raised a hand to quiet us. Then in a voice too loud for the microphone, said, 'Rubbish.' She cleared her throat. 'I'm disappointed to learn that some of you have been littering the school grounds.' Her t's were a hard tap against metal and her s's sounded like an angry cat. 'Just today,' she said, 'just today I found all kinds of rubbish behind the canteen. Empty packets of Twisties and Cheezoz.'

Everyone pissed themselves. One of the younger boys stuck his hand up and yelled, 'They're called Cheezles, Miss.'

'Cheezos, Cheezles, it doesn't matter. The point is that chips are a privilege.' In the front row of the assembly, little hands shot up. *What does that mean?* the Grade Ones wanted to know. 'A privilege,' Mrs Gogniat told them, 'is something you have to earn. Something that can be taken away from you if you aren't good.'

Zena said: 'Who gives a rat's. Salty-plums are better anyway.' She tugged at my ponytail. 'Let me play with your hair.' I shifted in front and positioned myself between her legs. Her fingers raked my skull, gently at first and then fast. 'Okay done,' she said. 'Now you do me.' We swapped places and she pulled off her scrunchie. Her hair was long and black and reached her bum. Zena once told me that her mum rubbed coconut oil into both of their scalps at night. I asked my mum to buy me some and came to school the next day with greasy tendrils stuck to my forehead and neck. 'I should've washed it better,' I said. Zena had laughed: 'It doesn't work on hair like yours.' I knew what she meant. My hair was too thin, too lank.

Zena's mother also smelt of coconut oil but on her the scent was mysterious and grownup. Like Zena, she was slightly built and pretty and dark. She worked as a nurse and wore a gold chain around her neck with a little Jesus pinned to a cross. I didn't know who Zena's real father was but she had a step-dad called Mick. The one time I went over to Zena's house I saw him beached on the couch, shirtless. His shorts made a V around his groin and he had an enormous belly like Tiddalick the Frog who we'd read about at school. When he went out, Zena said we should have a smoke – we could pinch one from her old man. We were playing Barbies at the time, and I rotated my doll's arms above her head. 'Won't Mick be home soon? Or your mum?' I wanted to know. 'Not for ages,' Zena said. She grabbed me by the hand and pulled me to the room where her parents slept. It was musty with cigarette smoke and something I hadn't smelt before. Above the double bed were posters of women. Women fondling their naked breasts, their shiny mouths open. Women clutching the space between their legs. I turned away so Zena wouldn't see my face. I couldn't imagine my mother in a room like this.

From the row behind me in the assembly area came the blast of an aerosol can. Toxic vanilla. It lingered in the atmosphere and I sneezed. Zena looked back at the older girls – quickly, before they could tell her off – and then leaned over to me and said in a low hiss, 'Impulse.' I nodded. We would wear it next year. Next year, we would be in Grade Seven and the other kids would look up to us and the teachers would respect us. The oldest kids in the school.

Mrs Gogniat was still talking. 'As this is the last assembly for the term, we have a treat for you. Some of you may know Anna de Silva. She graduated from our school four years ago. Anna is a dancer. And she's here to perform for us today. I want you to give her a very warm welcome.' We shifted on our bums. 'Give her your loudest clap,' Mrs Gogniat ordered. She tucked her microphone under her arm and started the applause. We joined in and she retreated.

We were still clapping when the sound of a guitar blasted from the speakers. Not slow strumming-by-the-campfire music, but frenetic and wild. I forgot about the other kids and as the music got faster I closed my eyes. When I opened them there was a girl onstage. Tall and slim, she wore the most extravagant dress, with ruffles of yellow and red. The girl raised her arms, waited a moment, and then danced. She twirled and clicked her high-heeled shoes on the wooden stage floor. She spun around like it was the most important thing – the only thing – she had to do. The music stopped suddenly and so did the girl. When it started again she retreated, her back towards us, making us miss her. My heart skittered and at last she turned to face us. She advanced across the stage, lifting her skirt so high I got a glimpse of her black underpants. Round and round she went and her skirt went up and down. The music didn't propel her, she propelled it, and as she spun around the space in my chest got bigger. Lighter. It was a weird feeling, like a bit of the dancer had gotten inside me. How did she do that; I wanted to know. And then a part of me spoke up and said: *Maybe one day you can do it too. Make people feel like this.*

'Huh.' Zena prodded me. When I didn't answer she said, 'Mick reckons girls like that are prickteasers. Because you can look but you can't touch.'

A gluggy feeling lodged in my stomach, like whenever I ate too much ice-cream at the pool. I thought of Mick and his posters and his enormous belly like a frog. I thought of those women stuck to the walls of his room. The way they had watched us as Zena smoked a cigarette and I pretended to take a drag, the stink of it lingering on my fingers.

Now, I looked at the girl onstage, and she was still dancing, still beautiful, but something was different. On the bench, the teachers whispered to each other. Some of them frowned. Behind me, the Grade Sevens were losing it. The boys started it and then the popular girls joined in, laughing and saying things I didn't want to hear. Zena passed me her scrunchie and told me to tie up her hair. I tossed it back in her lap.

Onstage, the girl lifted her skirt and let it fall and then she spun around once more, a swirl of red and yellow and black.

35

Deep in the Bowls of Chewton

Jock Read-Hill

It was a gentrified Friday in East Brunswick and the locals were hungry again. Amid the searing meat and bubbling oil I gazed dreamily out the small porthole window separating me from the rest of the world. My fantasies of life after work were interrupted by a set of blue eyes staring back through the porthole like a curious patron coming to witness the circus sideshow.

It was Keith, the partner of a fine friend of mine, someone I like very much but have little to do with. While happy to see him, when the head of a bald Irishman starts floating around the window beckoning for your attention, it's hard not to assume trouble. Little did I know he was the first of three wise Irishmen who would accompany me on this mad journey.

Without a greeting, Keith put a hand on my shoulder and said: 'Heard your Da used to play road bowls. I'm bringing up a crew to Chewton on Sunday. You're comin'.'

And that was that.

On the Saturday, I began to seriously wonder what I'd signed up for. It was true – my dad had played road bowls, but that was when I was young enough that crapping my pants in pubic was socially acceptable. That time was long gone and my father long passed with it.

On the vague premise of more the merrier, I collared the phone and called my brother. Though living nearby in Chewton and clearly happy to hear the words "road bowls" again, his yes to the Sunday was as solid as a castle made of jelly.

The crack of a Sunday mid-morning rolled around and I was standing out the front of home as Keith's four-door utility truck arrived. Riding shotgun was the second wise Irishman, Jakob: a handsome, bearded, sandy-haired chap with boy-next-door looks and the ability to keep such a straight face you could only tell by the glee in his eyes that he was having you on.

'You right mate?' He said, shaking hands. It had been some time since we'd last spoke. 'How many slabs we need?'

It was going to be that kind of day. My keep-cup was out of fashion.

'Just gettin' the fourth,' said Keith, clearly the designated driver.

We ventured into the northern suburbs of Melbourne, through the thin roads of modern cottages in various states of renovation. We came a stop out front of one with a nice green fence and there was a quick phone call with a minimal number of expletives. A minute later, Fern, the last wise Irishman of our group emerged, loping up his own path. He slid into the truck beside me.

'I was on the throne finishing a spliff when you called. Good craic! How many slabs we need?' Said Fern and off we went. He was the tallest of us with a permanent grin that varied in size depending on whether he was listening or telling a joke; the grin always grew to Cheshire cat proportions when hearing one. Now that we had the fellowship, the plan was simple and unclear. Get to the Red Hill and it will all work out.

It's a curious thing to sit in a confined space with three people who are in good spirits, of great wit and clearly catch up often. Rapid-fire inside jokes, political comments on the state of Ireland and chatter about workplaces I'd never known about ricocheted about the cabin, punctuated by the hissing of another beer opening and calls of 'Good craic' from Fern. I laughed at the appropriate times and spent the rest trying to keep up.

'So what's goin?' Fern asked me while the fine scenery of the Hume highway was pushed past the window.

I delivered a brief rundown of the homestead: that it was an old, small mining town and the Red Hill pub, around longer than any of us had been alive, remained nestled among the goldfields of central Victoria. It had been many years since strolling around its quiet streets or wandering bush-wise to make a game of dodging covered mineshafts. Mind you, he just wanted to know how to play road bowls.

Truth was, I had no idea. You tossed heavy disc up and down a road for all I could remember.

'Like Bullets?' he asked, opening another bottle.

After some confusion, it turned out Bullets was a similar game played in Ireland where cannonballs were pegged about for fun.

'Sure.' I said. None of us were.

We left the highway and cruised the perilous road of Tunnel Hill, a place where the damage from human hands still hides beneath the surface of the bush. Past the gathering of small pines, the marker for the graveyard turnoff. Keith pulled up when the only building of the correct pub size rose before us.

'Clouds are lookin' shite,' he said, vocalising our thoughts as he put a beanie on his head and the rest of us were obliged to stare skyward and nod in sage agreement.

The pub had changed. Gone were the misaligned floorboards, replaced with varnished hardwood. Gone was the seedy backroom pool table, now a restaurant of delicious smells. And gone was the old Arabian nights themed one arm bandit and it's blinking lights that kept me enchanted for longer than was healthy. The death of nostalgia had a selection of craft-beers for a headstone.

Stepping inside violated a part of my being that I still can't quite articulate.

We were the only customers, so we followed our plan and waited for someone else to show up and tell us what to do.

At first there were a few older patrons sidling in. Whether they were fellow road-bowlers or not was answered quickly by Jakob and his gregarious ways immediately asking that exact question and delighted to find that they were Irish nationals as well.

Like the start of a flood, more folk came in and the barmen began to move with purpose. I sat among the throng, recognising no one, delighted to spectate. Smiles were the oddly infectious variety yet didn't manage to infect me.

Rapidly, it became clear that the entirety of the customers were road bowls enthusiast and there wasn't one under the age of fifty. This was the old guard of the hippy migration to Chewton from the 1970s. The people who would've surrounded my parents when I was born with well-wishes and laughter that ever-excreting babies seem to provoke in adults. They didn't know that, and I couldn't find a polite way to mention it.

A fact that wouldn't remain hidden with the arrival of my brother from his fort out in Golden Point. Older than me, enough to know the names of most of this mob, it took three seconds for him to rightfully let on. The infectious smiles all swivelled my way then, a curious mix of joy and the sadness of time passing while they watched my features for similarities to their departed friend.

And like that, I was in a room full of comrades I'd never met.

Before anyone got too deep in their pints, Keith had done the sensible thing and figured out what was happening.

'There's a wee ride up the road, and then back to the fire station. You know where that is?'

'Sure.' I lied, hoping the fog of midday booze would lift enough for me to recall.

The cars started the same time as the sleet and we all packed in. The water encased the green hills of Chewton in a haze and the procession rumbled through it, back to the small group of pines near Tunnel Hill. We all turned onto the white gravel road of the Chewton Cemetery. We joined the other cars on the rise at the far end of the field, in the furthest corner where cultivation met the gum trees. My attention immediately drawn to a carved slot of granite that marked my fathers' final space. It struck me as oddly perverse that so many relative strangers would be traipsing about the graves.

Time had not been kind to many of the markers here, but the dozen we now surrounded were well cared for. The rosemary planted on my dad's plot had grown high in the time I'd been absent and now covered the ancient road bowl that lurked within the fronds. I picked a sprig and pocketed it after rolling the savoury herb between my fingers, placing a kiss on the sap and touching the top of his headstone. From the corner of my eye I noticed more of the same weighted smiles at my own little observance of time.

Many glasses were stacked on an old stump and the bottles of port emerged. We hugged ourselves against the soft rain while the glasses were filled. The ringleader of the procession, the Irish Captain, spoke gentle words about friends no longer with us. The glasses were refilled, and songs were invited to be sung. A songstress stepped forward.

There is a quality in Irish ballads that is seldom found elsewhere especially in the one that was sung then: a finality, an acceptance of struggle and an understanding of grief that is seldom expressed so poignantly. It sent each listener to a place all of their own, the place where we all meditate upon the fickleness of mortality and the grim certainty that we would join the dead in good time.

My brother, the wisemen and myself seemed the only attendees that didn't know the words, or at least, weren't ready to start singing along.

'Time for the game,' The Irish captain said and like a spell, the cheer resurfaced and we piled back in. The last I saw of that sober hill was the headstone opposite my fathers's one of his best pals laid alongside him: 'Randall Percy – He loved good craic.'

While that cemetery might've been a sober place, I most certainly was not. I heroically led the wisemen a clean past the fire station and nearly to the next town before turning us around. The Chewton fire department is a squat shed, far more pragmatic than beautiful, and located right near the pub. A coincidence, I thought not.

We arrived fashionably late, enough that the teams had already been decided upon. The Paddys versus Chewton. The Irish Captain was, oddly enough, captain of the Paddys. Due to my brother claiming injury (one brought about by Guinness, ironically) he'd now be scoring. The captaincy of Chewton now fell to me. It's a good start to a game when a captain and the scorekeeper don't know how to play. Suddenly the weight was on my shoulders. It didn't help when I asked and the Irish Captain told me the rules penned in 1970 by my father and his rascal associates.

'Rule number one,' he said impishly. 'Chewton must always win.'

This brought about plenty of guffawing, so much that I never got to hear the second rule. My brother had been given a crash course and he safely intercepted me before play.

The port was interfering with recollection here but the gist of it was this: two teams compete in tossing a road bowl up and down an allocated course, whichever team made it back in the fewest shots won. Simple, efficient and according to Fern, exactly like Bullets from Ireland. The difference being that the Irish were sensible enough to use a ball, my forebears had chosen a four-pound weight instead. If you've never seen one of these devils, it's a hand-sized disc with a tapered edge so you don't know where the bugger will fly off to when it hits the ground.

With much aplomb I threw the first shot of the game. The little white-gravel path that started the course teetered down to a brook and across a narrow bridge. The awkward bowl left my hand, flipping forwards instead of the planned curved roll. It spun once, twice and a third time before hitting the gravel, righting itself despite what physics might've implied, and curved gently across the bridge to much applause.

'That was easy,' I distinctly remember saying, a comment I would clearly come to regret.

The Paddys cleared the bridge in one throw too and on the game went. Our band of mostly greys caroused up the gravel through the piddling rain, pausing only to call out the next player, comment on similarities between the countryside and the emerald isles or for the wheelbarrow full of beer to catch up.

Due to a shortage of home-grown competitors, Jakob and Fern had been forced to become turncoats and play for the wicked Chewtoners and their port-riddled Ahab, already convinced of rule one and now yearning to take a harpoon to the Paddys.

Locals who heard the commotion stood on their porches and watched as the gleeful caravan wandered by. Several spectators were treated to the shot of the match when the drunken Chewton captain threw such a mighty, lopsided bowl that it collided with the Graveyard Songstress before careening into a ditch, costing the team precious points while I scrabbled in the dirt looking for it.

More than a little humbled, I gave the supply wheelbarrow a wide berth.

The game marched on, with nearly everyone having their go at those unwieldy weights and laughing no matter what happened after. The final, and spectacular shot came from Fern. A brilliant bowl that managed to roll all the way around him and back to the point he'd thrown it. It was just far enough to count. While the shot petered out, the cheering didn't and what was left in the wheelbarrow was seized. My brother tallied the score.

Chewton lost by a point.

Deep in my sodden and sotted mind I entertained the notion that there were traitors in the ranks, that perhaps Jakob was joking a little too much. A suspicion compounded when the trophy emerged. A big, heavy bastard of a thing with a road bowl ensconced on top like a fat king and a list of all the previous winners etched in. The Paddys had won every single game for the last fifteen years.

On the wet lawn of Chewton, I stood side by side with the Irish Captain, each holding a side of the trophy grinning like fools for the camera and only then did I understand. It was a ritual, much more complicated than my rosemary frippery. It didn't matter who won, it didn't matter who showed up. It mattered that the game was played. Not necessarily fairly, but it must be played.

The empty wheelbarrow was returned to the Red Hill, followed swiftly by the rest of us. Not long after I was quietly trying to stop the rotation of the earth with my iron grip on the bar when Keith mimed the driving of a car at me. With the final act in the observance of road bowls completed, our duty was done.

With promises of next year, we went back to Melbourne, the speakers flowing with the greatest Irish songs of all time as dictated by Jakob, and the lyrics courteously butchered by the rest of us, stopping only once to make sure a manicured hedge in the Northern suburbs got a fine hosing down.

The wise men departed. I sat at home, swore off port forever and mused on the spiritual weight that four pounds can give and slept, rosemary still on my fingers.

Contributors

Editors

Rebecca Bryson is a writer, researcher and editor who is currently completing a PhD in Creative Writing at Monash University. After having worked in the publishing industry for eight years, she threw caution to the wind and decided to delve into the creative side of the writing game. She has an interest in speculative fiction and her research is centred on the future of technology from a Marxist feminist perspective. Her creative work has been published in *The Suburban Review* and her short story 'Infinite Scroll' was commended by the judges of the 2019 AAWP/ASSF Emerging Writer's Prize 2019.

Benjamin Jay is a writer and editor for a number of interdisciplinary journals in the Literary and Cultural Studies Graduate Research Program at Monash University, where he is currently completing a PhD in Creative Writing. His research focus is on representations of homosexuality and neurodiversity in children's and young adult fiction.

Giulia Mastrantoni is currently completing a PhD at Monash University. Her research investigates how to better represent sexual violence in fiction, nonfiction, and creative nonfiction. She is co-editor-in-chief of *Colloquy*, a committee member for the Victorian Postgraduate Criminology Conference, and a published author. Giulia's fiction in Italian has been featured on a number of literary blogs, and it has won the international prize Napoli Cultural Classic (2015), whereas Giulia's fiction in English has been featured on SWAMP (2019) and on Litinfinite (2020). Giulia presented her work at Falling Walls Lab (Melbourne 2019) and at NeMLA (Boston 2020).

Authors

Sarah Arber is a mother and second-year undergraduate arts student at Monash University. Sarah takes a keen interest in women's issues; it is her hope to shine a light on the many facets of the female experience within modern society.

Alison Bernasconi is a keen reader, but an accidental writer. She has written song lyrics, music, poetry and short stories for small audiences, and for herself. Recently, she has started on more substantial fictional work. She loves using words to advocate, create, and represent, and to explore the common and the uncommon in people.

Richie Black is an AWGIE-winning writer. His credits include plays *The Inspection* (Old 505), *Violent Extremism and Other Adult Party Games* (Ain't It Fun), *The Local* (Insomniac Theatre) and the comedy web series *Toxic Kiss: Achtung Mein Kunst*. He graduated from NIDA in 2016 with an MFA (Writing).

JR Burgmann is a writer, editor, researcher and PhD candidate at Monash University, where he also teaches and is a member of the Climate Change Communication Research Hub. His PhD focusses on climate change communication and narrative representations of climate change. His research areas include Literary Studies, Media Studies, and Australian Indigenous Studies.

Joan Cahill's poetry has been published in anthologies including *fourW*, *Short and Twisted* and FAW Queensland's *Brio 2016*. She won the Melbourne Poets Union's *Urban Realism Award* 2012, and 2013 FAW Regional's *Vibrant Verse* First Prize. Her first poetry collection *Buddha's Left Foot* was published in 2016.

Derek Chan is a current undergraduate student at Monash University, and has won multiple university prizes for his writing. His works are forthcoming in Australian literary journals such as *Cordite Poetry Review*.

Miguela Considine is a Filipino-Australian writer based in Sydney, whose stories always end up darker than she initially intends. With a background in PR in the tech and games industry, she has a special interest in exploring mental and chronic illness through speculative fiction.

Leah De Forest lives in Boston and studies fiction at the Warren Wilson College MFA Program for Writers. Her novel was longlisted for the 2015 Richell Prize and highly commended in the 2013 Victorian Premier's unpublished manuscript award. She's written for *Overland*, *The Canberra Times*, *Kill Your Darlings* and *Eureka Street*.

Jane Downing has poetry and prose published around Australia and overseas including in *Griffith Review*, *Antipodes*, *Southerly*, *Island*, *Westerly*, *Canberra Times*, *Cordite*, *Best Australian Poems* (2004 & 2015) and previously in *Verge*. A collection of her poetry entitled *When Figs Fly* was published by Close-Up Books in 2019.

Merav Fima is a PhD candidate in the Literary and Cultural Studies Program at Monash University. Her prose and poetry have appeared in a number of anthologies and literary journals, including: *Israel Short Stories*; *Living Legacies: A Collection of Writing by Contemporary Canadian Jewish Women*; *VOICES: Poetry from Israel and Abroad*; *Poetica Magazine*; and *Parchment: A Journal of Contemporary Canadian Jewish Writing*. Her short story 'Bride Immaculate' won the first prize in the Energheia Literary Competition in Matera, Italy.

Yanping Gao is a PhD candidate in LLCL in the Arts Faculty in Monash University, and is an amateur in literature writing. Now she is involved in the literary and cultural program.

Carolyn Gerrish is a Sydney poet. She has published five collections of poetry. The last one was *The View from the Moon* (Island Press, 2011). She enjoys performing her work and is currently working on her sixth collection.

Sue Goodall is an emerging writer of short fiction and poetry. She convenes the Women Writers Network – an all genres open writing group at Writing NSW. Her short story 'Grammerly Correctish' was performed at Little Fictions in the Sydney Writers Festival 2019.

Ben Grech is a teacher and aspiring writer who lives in Melbourne with his wife and seven-month old daughter. He has recently completed his Honours in Creative Writing at Monash University and his work has appeared in *Page Seventeen*.

Pip Griffin is a Sydney poet. She has two collections, *Salt Lake* (2004), *Last Song (the first year)* (2007) and two verse novels, *Ani Lin: the journey of a Chinese Buddhist nun* (2010) and *Margaret Caro: the extraordinary life of a pioneering dentist in New Zealand 1848–1938* (2020), all published by Pohutukawa Press. Her poems and short stories have appeared in journals and anthologies.

Angela Jones is a writer, musician, artist and academic from Perth. She is a PhD candidate in Monash University's writing program and a published author in the fields of popular cultural studies and education. Her true love is telling a tale of whim or weaving a lyrical riff.

Rachel Martin is a Melbourne writer and member of Inner City Writers. She has a background working in science and also teaching ESL, was long-listed for The Australian/Vogel's Literary Award, has published adult comics and short stories (including in a London Anthology of bisexual erotica) and is working on her second novel.

Ben Mason's short fiction has been performed, published and awarded, including in Brain drip, and StyleUsLit (upcoming) KSP writing comp, and Lit Live Perth. His collection of short fiction was long-listed for the 2019 Fogarty Award. He will be a 2020 writer in residence at Mattie Furphie House for the Fellowship of Australian Writers WA.

Magdalena McGuire is an award-winning writer who was born in Poland, grew up in the tropics of Northern Australia, and now lives in Melbourne. She is undertaking a PhD in Creative Writing at Monash University.

Anna McShane-Potts is an emerging writer from Hobart, currently living in Melbourne and completing her BA in literary studies and BCom in behavioural commerce at Monash University. Anna's writing explores the human condition, our complex relationship with nature, and the flexibility of perception.

Callum Methven is a twenty-four-year-old writer from Bunyip, Victoria, who enjoys writing about the swamp he grew up in and anything else that makes him nostalgic.

Fiona Murphy is a Deaf poet and essayist. Her work has appeared in *Kill Your Darlings*, *Griffith Review*, *Overland*, *Big Issue*, *The Lifted Brow*, amongst others. In 2019, she was awarded the Overland Fair Australia essay prize.

Kerrin O'Sullivan is a Melbourne-based writer with a love of words and faraway places. Her short fiction has been published in various literary magazines, her travel features in The *Weekend Australian*, *The Age* and *Jetstar Inflight*. She was a 2016 Wheeler Centre Hot Desk Fellow for short fiction. www.kerrinosullivan.com.

Jackson C. Payne is a short story writer from Aotearoa-New Zealand. His work has appeared in *NZ Author*, *Spinoff*, and *Newsroom*, and a short documentary he wrote, 'Candy's Crush', is being screened at film festivals around the world. Jackson has just begun his PhD in Creative Writing at Monash University.

Vanessa Proctor is the Immediate Past President of the Australian Haiku Society. Her poetry has appeared in journals such as *Australian Poetry Journal*, *Island*, *Meanjin* and *Southerly*, and has also been carved in stone, printed on teabag labels and set to music.

Jock Read-Hill is an RMIT Professional Writing and Editing alumni currently plying his trade over the streets of Brunswick East. He enjoys legitimate criticism, extreme lounging and blundering around in the dark.

Ava Redman is a student in her third year at Western Sydney University, majoring in Journalism. She has been working as a freelance writer and self-publishing works along the way. She has recently started working in film and producing scripts across various genres and hopes to create a pilot show this year.

Victor Chrisnaa Senthinathan is currently a fifth-year undergraduate medical student at Monash University. His writing aims to explore ideas like the macroscopic and microscopic dynamics of being a second-generation immigrant in Australia, as well as the power imbalances within relationships such as the parent and child. He has also been longlisted for the Liminal Prize.

Olivia Shenken is a student at Monash University, currently completing a Bachelor of Arts. She is interested in speculative fiction with an empathetic touch. Her work has appeared in *F*EMS Zine*, *Lot's Wife*, and *Incisors & Grinders*. Somehow, warm cups of tea keep spontaneously appearing in her writing.

Jeanne Viray is a Manila-born writer based in Melbourne. Her work has appeared in *Voiceworks*, *Verge: Uncanny*, *F*EMSZINE*, *DjedPress*, *Lot's Wife*, and *Incisors & Grinders*. She has completed a Bachelor of Arts and is currently studying law. She writes experimental and speculative pieces. She likes iced tea, fairytales, and mimicking voices.

Michael Walton is an emerging queer writer, editor and spoken word performer based in Melbourne. They are studying physics, literature and archaeology at Monash University. Their work, both poetry and prose, has appeared in the anthology *Verge: Uncanny*, the magazine *Lot's Wife* and in the student publication *Incisors & Grinders*.

Les Wicks has toured widely and seen publication across 29 countries in 15 languages. His 14th book of poetry is *Belief* (Flying Islands, 2019). http://leswicks.tripod.com/lw.htm.

Ziyang Zhang is currently an international student completing a Master of Creative Writing at the University of Sydney. He has previously studied Literary Studies (English Literature and Creative Writing) at undergraduate level with honours at Monash University. He is interested in feminism and stylistic analysis.